BROWNING BATTLES ON

BROWNING BATTLES ON

Peter Corris

ISBN-10: 0207176132
ISBN-13: 9780207176135

For Tom Thompson

For help in the preparation of this book the writer wishes to thank Jean Bedford, Mr John McCallum, Dr Stewart Firth and the staff of the National Film & Sound Archive.

CHAPTER ONE

Someone once told me that Ghengis Khan was at war for the whole of his life. I don't imagine he lived as long as I have, but even so it's a frightening thought. I've been in three or four wars, one way and another, and I can't say I have pleasant memories of them. Swaggering about in uniform with money in your pockets and the girls giving you the eye is all right, but there's precious little of that compared with square-bashing, brass-polishing, saluting officers and picking lice out of your pubic hair. That's my experience anyway. But what's even worse than being a soldier is being a civilian, a non-combatant, and being *taken* for a soldier, and an enemy at that.

In August 1944 it looked as if I was set to enjoy the latter part of World War II about a hundred times more than I'd enjoyed World War I, say, or the Mexican Revolution. I was flying from California to Australia, togged up as a US army captain, looking forward to a very rapid promotion. I was cast as an Australian general in a propaganda film to be entitled 'South Pacific Showdown'. Except that there wasn't going to be a film—it was all an elaborate charade got up between the War Department and some Hollywood patriots. What I'd actually be doing was providing a smokescreen behind which a *real* propaganda film was being made. Still, it promised to be a soft billet for Dick Kelly, which was the name I'd be going under—good hotels, ample food and drink, plenty of bowing and scraping and a decent pay cheque at the end of it.[1]

Things came badly unstuck when the B52 crashed during a rainstorm, killing everyone on board but me. I scrambled out of the wreckage into a reeking jungle and punctured my skin in a hundred places scrambling through the bush to get clear of the plane. It didn't explode but, just as I was giving thanks for that, I fell into the hands of a dozen or so soldiers of Nippon. Not one of them stood over five foot four or weighed more than eight stone—in fact they were looking pretty famished, but they'd kept their bayonets shiny bright and all seemed anxious to test the sharpness on my hide. I threw up my hands and babbled that I was a friend with a great admiration for their Emperor, although I was damned if I could remember his name at that precise moment.

They surrounded me, jabbering away and thrusting with their bayonets as if they were each trying to pick a tender spot. It was dark and raining but one of the Japanese carried a big flashlight which he tried to keep trained on my face. I was ducking away from the pigstickers so much he had a hard job doing it and in the wavering beam I caught glimpses of their faces and the dense jungle all around us. We were in a small clearing, flattening it as we moved and I was pretty sure that clearing was going to be my burial place.

'Don't kill me,' I said. 'I surrender. Prisoner of war. Geneva Convention.'

One of the bayonets, held more steadily than the others, came to rest just below my Adam's apple. I looked down at the shiny steel and then slowly looked along the length of the rifle barrel up into the face of my executioner. He wore thick glasses with metal rims and he had gold fillings in his teeth. I could see the teeth because he was smiling.

'I hope you've got some cigarettes on you, buddy,' he said. 'Some of these pals of mine are ready to kill for a smoke.'

'What?'

'You heard me. Don't act so surprised. How do you think a Jap houseboy knows when to open the door and wash the car if he can't speak American?'

I still couldn't take it in. 'I'm not an American.'

'No?' The tip of the bayonet sliced through my tie, which had slipped down a few inches. 'You look like a US army captain to me, sir!'

The 'sir!' was pure mockery and the bayonet was back at my throat. 'I'm an Australian.'

'Yeah? Like Errol Flynn?'

There was probably nothing else he could have said that would have caused me to do what I did next. I pulled back a fraction, grabbed the barrel and hammered the rifle butt into his chest. He gasped and reeled back, leaving me holding the weapon. Wrong way round, of course, and with a dozen or so rifles pointing at my head, but still . . .

The English-speaker recovered fast. He grabbed back his rifle. 'You've got balls.'

'I've also got cigarettes,' I said. 'Probably a couple of hundred cartons. Tell that to your pals.'

He spoke rapidly but the news didn't seem to swing the meeting in my favour.

'They're not impressed, buddy. We saw the B52 come down. We can find it in the morning. The feeling is, who needs you?'

'The plane's booby-trapped.' The idea, no doubt picked up from some movie or other, jumped into my head and I came straight out with it. Very convincing, but a good line needs a good piece of movement to back it up. Like all heavy smokers I always carried two packs. I undid the flap on my jacket pocket, reached in and pulled out my Camels. The next thing I knew an umbrella had opened and I was standing under it. Eager hands were reaching out for the cigarettes. I produced my Zippo and lit maybe ten cigarettes. The soldiers stood around in the rain, puffing and cupping the smokes in their hands.

'Not having one yourself, Captain?'

'Dick Kelly's my name. I'm a civilian. I figure I might need them for something more important, like saving my life. Who're you?'

'Sergeant Haruki Kaminaga. Bet you can't guess what my employers called me in Honolulu?'

'Harry?'

'You got it, Dick. I never did like that.'

That's the way it is in dangerous situations, the danger ebbs and flows, comes from different directions. The soldiers were enjoying their cigarettes and there couldn't have been more than three or four rifles pointing at me, but now Harry the houseboy seemed to be recalling past insults and slights. Here was his chance to get back at the people who owned the houses, cars and pools. He took off his glasses and wiped the water away with a piece of cloth. I noticed for the first time how down-at-heel these guys were. Their uniforms were crumpled, muddy rags; their boots were gaping and they all looked in need of a good feed. Only their weapons were well maintained.

Harry replaced his specs. There was some stirring amongst the lower ranks and I put the Camel packet into the fist of the biggest of them—a bantamweight who looked as if he could fight at nine stone if he got a few bowls of rice inside him.

'Harry,' I said. 'The B52's loaded with smokes, booze and food, all of which you guys seem to need. Let's be friends.'

'You're doing it. Calling me Harry.'

'You can call me Dick.'

He laughed. 'Dick. Yeah, that's another thing. I don't suppose you've got any women on board?'

I shook my head. 'No women, and everyone's dead but me. Where the hell are we?'

He stared at me through his clean lenses. 'That was going to be my next question to you.'

'Shit, you mean you don't know?'

The other soldiers got tired of standing around in the rain listening to a foreign language. They muttered. The bantamweight muttered loudly. Harry did what any smart sergeant does—he did what his men wanted to do while making it look like his idea. He rapped out a few orders and I found myself slogging through the bush, four back from the man with the flashlight and a machete who was lighting and clearing our way. The umbrella had disappeared. I was soaked to the skin, but I only felt the poke of a bayonet once or twice. That's probably OK under the Geneva Convention.

After about fifteen minutes walk we came to a small clearing in the jungle, not a natural clearing, but one that had been hacked out by hand. Several large fires were burning and in their light I could see a huge shape looming up behind the camp. It was grey and mostly covered by branches and vines that had been thrown over it. Through the camouflage, small patches gleamed dully in the light from the fires.

'That's our kite,' Harry said. 'Mitsubishi bomber. Came down a month ago.'

'Rainstorm? Lightning strike?'

'Yeah, instruments went haywire.'

We were standing outside an improvised shelter, a tarpaulin draped over a rough wooden frame. Harry's voice dropped to a whisper. 'This could be a bit rough for you, buddy. Stick to the booby-trap story and you might be OK.'

A man emerged from the shelter. He was slightly taller than the other Japanese and not as thin. His uniform was better cut and in better nick. An officer, getting the best of everything available, if ever I saw one. He spat out an order and a rifle butt hit me behind the knees. I sank to the ground and kept my head down, looking at the officer's polished boots. Above me, a brisk conversation was going on between Harry and the officer with an occasional comment from other parties. I heard fingers snapping and risked a glance upwards. The bantam-weight handed the now pretty deflated Camel pack to the officer. You've seen one army in action, you've seen them all.

There was a hissing sound and I looked up again. The officer had drawn a long sword with a slightly curved blade from a scabbard. With the firelight winking on it, the blade seemed to glow. I was instantly sorry for every unkind act I'd ever done, every mean thought. I was about to start babbling for mercy when Harry's beach-boy drawl lightened a moment that badly needed lightening.

'Lieutenant Okano here is a prize asshole who doesn't speak English,' Harry said. 'He's uncomfortable because a lowly NCO like me does. If he gets uncomfortable enough he's likely to order your head removed. Be a good idea for you to drop that head a bit lower if you want to keep it. I wouldn't go so far as to lick his boots, but you get my drift.'

I bowed lower.

The sword touched the back of my neck. I waited to hear the intake of breath that would accompany the upward swing. There was nothing I could do. You can't move fast from a kneeling position. I could duck but that was likely to have nasty side effects. What Joe Louis said about Billy Conn flashed into my mind: 'He can run, but he can't *hide*'.[2]

Then the lieutenant was talking. Harry spoke. The lieutenant became angry. *Thanks a lot, Harry*, I thought. Harry remained calm. The sword was resting on my neck now and if I hadn't had thick, wavy hair back there it would have been cutting me. My mind was numb. I could feel and hear things. My eyes were clenched shut. The rain stopped. Then the slight weight was lifted and I heard the whispering sound of its being re-sheathed. I breathed out slowly and took another breath in. A sweet one, that, a bonus breath.

'He buys the booby-trap story, so you can look forward to tomorrow. You can ask a question, but keep it humble.'

'After you get the goodies from the B52, then what?'

'That's something you and me'll have to talk about. OK, get up and give him a salute. Try not to look six foot two while you're doing it.'

I saluted Lieutenant Okano from a crouch. He sniffed, turned smartly and ducked back inside his shelter. Harry jabbed me with his bayonet.

'Did I just hit a bible or a flask?'

'Flask,' I said.

'Thought so. Let's find us a dry place to drink in.'

We repaired to a spot close to the fuselage of the plane. Harry barked some orders and a fire was quickly built and lit. We squatted down with our backs to a group of soldiers who were playing some kind of dice game. My clothes steamed in the warmth of the fire. Harry took out a pistol and put it on a rock near his right hand.

'Got any more butts, Dick?'

I produced the other pack. Harry ripped it open and tossed half the contents to the dice players. They grunted their appreciation. I took a cigarette myself and offered the pack to Harry.

He shook his head. 'I got enough vices. Speaking of which . . .'

I lit up and took out my hip flask. In it was about half a pint of Early Times bourbon—'sippin' whisky' as the good ol' boys call it, also talking whisky. Harry took a slug and let out a sigh of satisfaction.

'Better,' he said. 'Much better. Enough of that stuff and I could forget I'm sitting in a stinking jungle, the fuck knows where, with a bunch of assholes looking for ways to get themselves killed. Present company excluded, of course.'

I took a tiny sip. 'Right. Have another drink.'

'Don't mind if I do. I spotted you right off, Dick. It was in your eyes. You ain't no hero.'

He never said a truer word, but I couldn't let him walk all over me. 'The life I've led,' I said, 'if I was a hero I'd be dead.'

'Let's put our cards on the table. What's the most important thing on your mind right now?'

I was still feeling such relief at having my head on my shoulders that I hadn't done much thinking with it. But it wasn't a hard question to answer. 'Getting out of here in one piece.'

'Not winning the war, shit like that?'

'Hell, no. Well, I *hope* my side wins, but if it doesn't I'll just have to cope.'

Harry took another drink, wiped his glasses again and stared at me in frank admiration. 'You ever studied philosophy, Dick?'

I shook my head. My precious, still attached head.

'You appear to have a philosophy. Seems it goes something like, "the world doesn't exist if I'm not in it".'

'Well ...'

'I'm not knocking it. Don't get me wrong. You're my boy. Soon as I saw you I could feel a plan coming on. Have a little more bourbon.'

I did. I had a feeling I was going to need it. Planners can be dangerous people; some of them think that once the planning's over they've done their bit, and that leaves you to put the plan into operation. Fortunately, Harry was more of a consultative type. 'We both want to survive the war, right?'

'Right.'

'And neither one of us knows where the fuck we are, right?'

'Well, we know the general area. How did your lot get here?'

'We left New Ireland or New Britain, I never knew which one we were on, to go to the Philippines. They stripped the bomber and put a hundred or so of us on board.'

I looked around the camp. I could see perhaps twenty men grouped near the fires. There were bound to be sentries—say, six— plus Harry, plus the lieutenant in his pavilion. 'You lost a few.'

Harry nodded and finished the bourbon in one big swallow. He handed me the empty flask. 'Lost half when she crashed. We've sent out a couple of search parties since. No-one came back. We're down to twenty-three men not counting Okano, which I don't on account of he's no use for anything. He'd skewer me for telling you our strength, by the way.'

'I'll take it as a sign of trust. The B52's not booby-trapped.'

'Never figured it was, but thanks.'

It was a pity we didn't have any bourbon left to seal our mutual understanding. I was feeling tired after all the stress and strain. The whisky and the warmth of the fire made me drowsy and I yawned.

'I don't quite cotton to you, Dick,' Harry said. 'I had you pegged as slightly yellow, but you grabbed my rifle back there and now you're yawning like it's time for your nap.'

'I'm lazy,' I said. 'So where d'you reckon we are? Some place in New Guinea?'

'Most likely, which brings me back to my plan. Some parts of New Guinea are controlled by your side and some parts by mine, right?'

'That's right, last I heard. But we've got more of it.'

'So I'm a gambler.'

I was genuinely tired and having trouble following him. The ground we were stretched out on started to feel soft and even the rocks had a comfortable curve. 'I don't get you.'

Harry leaned closer and whispered, the way he always did when what he had to say mattered. 'This is my plan. We cut out of here tonight, you and me. We raid the B52 for supplies. If we run into my people, you're my prisoner. If we come across any of yours, vice versa. Whaddya say?'

'I'm tired. Not tonight.'

'Buddy, it *has* to be tonight. Believe me, you don't have any nights to spare.'

CHAPTER TWO

After a while a soldier who looked to be about twelve years old delivered Harry a disgusting-smelling mess in a tin dixie. Nothing for yours truly. Harry spooned it down in a second, belched and put the tin aside.

'Sago,' he said. 'You wouldn't be able to eat it. But I've gotta keep my strength up. The thing is, all the guys here are so weakend by starvation and illness that they fall asleep at the drop of a hat. Sentries'll be snoring before midnight. Stand up, Dick.'

I was half asleep myself and I thought Harry might be proposing a visit to the latrine which would have been welcome. I got creakily to my feet and he felled me with a blow to the neck, delivered with the side of his hand. He shouted as he struck and he kicked me in the ribs as I lay in the dirt.

'Moan a bit.'

I moaned.

Harry shouted again and a soldier came up carrying a length of rope. Harry trussed me up, rolled me on to my back and spat in my face. For a minute I thought he'd turned on me, then I saw the wink. A few soldiers gathered round and Harry jabbered at them. Harry had taken possession of the flashlight. He shone it on my wet face and made a remark which his comrades found very funny. Then everyone lost interest in me. The dice players went back to their game. Harry wrapped himself in a blanket and stretched out on the ground a few feet away. I lay there, with spittle drying on my face, my ribs hurting, scratches itching and with sundry other aches and pains. *What have I done to deserve this?* I thought. *I've never offered any offence to man or beast. Women maybe, but that was all a matter of hormones, beyond my control.*

I watched the stars in the sky, but I'm no countryman. I couldn't tell the time by them. All they told me was that we were in the southern hemisphere, and I already knew that.

Harry's whisper rose slightly above the noise of the jungle— dripping, rustling and creaking sounds. 'Be time to move soon. Give it ten minutes.'

'Great,' I said. 'I'll be totally numb by then. Won't feel a thing when you lift me up and carry me.'

He laughed softly. 'You're a laugh, Dick. Hold still.'

He slid his rifle towards me and cut the rope with the bayonet. I stretched my arms out at my sides and rotated my shoulders a little. Everything worked. Harry was still in a sleeping position. I was cold; the fire had died down. 'I'm sure the Geneva Convention says a prisoner should have a blanket.'

'Lieutenant Okano would use the Geneva Convention to wipe his ass, and then make you eat it. Be patient. This is the rest of your life you got on the line here.'

I wanted a cigarette and a piss. I wanted a hot drink with alcohol in it and a steak and a bed … I swallowed hard and tried to get a grip on myself. We were going to raid the B52. I could find a weapon and get clear of Harry. Then I could . . . The thought of wandering around in the jungle made me shiver. To stop my teeth chattering I said the first thing that came into my head.

'Were you really a houseboy in Honolulu?'

'Houseboy, taxi driver, pimp, anything that'd keep me out of the fields. Man, I hated field work.'

'How come you joined the army? Didn't you know it'd be more like field work than pimping, at least for an enlisted man?'

'Hah, hah. I like you, Dick. I dig your sense of humour. We're going to get along fine. Tell you the truth, I'd built up a bit of a hatred for the round-eyes. Spell in the Ohahu penitentiary helped that along. I hopped over to old Nippon to kick ass.'

'And?'

'I hear there's a Jap unit in the US army now. That so?'

'I don't know. Could be.'

'Way I shoulda gone. Maybe it's not too late to change sides, huh?'

I couldn't take much more of this. My head was swimming with possibilities of deception and deceit, and I was close to cramping up all along one side. 'If we're going, let's go,' I said.

Harry looked around cautiously. The fires had died down; men were asleep tucked in behind rocks and under makeshift canvas and leaf shelters. They had made screens out of branches and leaves and used them partly for protection from the cool air and partly, I guessed, as camouflage. Deep snores shuddered in the warm, moist air.

'OK,' Harry said. *'Banzai.'*

'What's that mean?'

'It means charge, but I mean creep on our bellies like snakes.'

That's exactly what we did—wriggled from our position near the plane, crawled past sleeping soldiers, crept through the jungle within feet of two snoring sentries and got clear of the camp. The night was dark but Harry used the flashlight sparingly to pick up the track we'd made coming through the bush a few hours back. Eventually we stopped. We'd been moving fast and I was dripping with sweat.

'This is where we found you. Where's the B52?'

'Jesus Christ, I don't know. I just ran away from the bloody thing. I don't even know what direction it's in.'

Harry had left his rifle in camp but not his bayonet. He slipped it from a scabbard strapped to his thigh and put it where it had been before, at the base of my throat. 'You'd better think about it, Dick.'

'I thought we were friends.'

'Sure we are, as long as we're useful to each other. Your useful-ness starts here. If you don't come through I might just have to claim I gutted you when you tried to escape.'

'Harry, I . . .'

He kept the blade near my throat and moved the flashlight beam around the clearing. 'Take a look. Must be something you remember.'

There wasn't a thing but I couldn't just stand there. I pretended to recognise a flattened bush and pointed at it. 'That way.'

We slogged through the jungle for what seemed like an hour. Stumbling through some undergrowth we disturbed a swarm of insects that buzzed angrily and bit me on the hands and face. I yelped and slapped at them.

'Shut up!' Harry hissed. 'They might be after us already.'

I ignored him. I was getting sick of this futile blundering about. I stopped. 'That'd bugger your plan, wouldn't it?'

'Not necessarily. You're not an officer, are you, Dick?'

'I told you. I'm a bloody civilian.'

'That's swell. If you were an officer, Okano'd be real mad that an enlisted man killed you. It's part of his code of conduct, see. Only an officer can execute an officer. But since that don't apply—'

'Harry—'

'You've got five fuckin' minutes to find that plane before I show you what your insides look like.'

I was facing him. Our heads were inches apart. I was ten inches taller and outweighed him by thirty pounds, but the bayonet made it a David and Goliath situation. I had to make a move, any kind of move, but the chances of having a windpipe to breathe through were small. I drew a deep breath.

'Sorry, Dick.'

'Wait.' The genuine urgency in my voice made him hesitate. 'What?'

I'd taken the breath in through my nostrils. 'I can smell something,' I said.

When someone says they can smell something the automatic response is to sniff. Harry did, and Harry was a non-smoker with a much keener sense of smell than me. There was a light breeze and Harry sniffed at it like a hunting dog.

'You're right,' he said. 'That's gasoline.'

'Aviation fuel.' I wet my finger and held it up into the breeze, taking care to ease away slightly from the bayonet as I did so. I pointed. 'That way.'

The bayonet slid back into its scabbard and Harry trained the flashlight in the direction I'd indicated. You could convince yourself that something had crashed through the bushes. Harry hared off, leaving me to follow, which I did, quick smart. He may have just offered to slit my throat, but in the middle of a pitch dark jungle a thousand miles from nowhere, you cling to whatever human companionship is available. We stumbled along, getting lashed in the face by creepers and tripping over tree roots. Harry hadn't had a decent feed for a month and I guess he could taste the food and drink. Whatever the reason, he set a cracking pace.

And there it was, perched up on a rock shelf like a giant beached whale. I could see the wing I'd jumped from and I wondered how I'd had the nerve to do it. It was a long way, maybe thirty feet, down to the bush I'd landed in so safely. The smell of fuel was strong and it worried me until I remembered the steady rain earlier in the night. If an electric spark or a piece of hot metal hadn't sent the whole thing sky-high by now, it was probably safe. The questions were, did Harry know that and, if not, could I turn the knowledge to my advantage.

'Thing's been soaked,' Harry said. 'Safe as a Waikiki cabana. Let's get up there.'

He began scrambling up the rocks, dodging around nimbly, using his torch beam to see the next foothold. There was no way

I could have made it. I didn't even want to try. The moon sailed clear of some clouds and the stars shone brightly. After floundering around in the dark for so long I was beginning to acquire reasonable night vision. I could see a way to get around the back of the plane and the rock shelf and I took it, brushing aside the damp branches and creepers. I worked my way back until I ran out of light. The overhead canopy was dense and cut visibility to zero.

I took the torn tie from around my neck, scrabbled on the jungle floor for a few sticks, tied them together and lit them with my Zippo. As a torch it wasn't much, but the light enabled me to continue until I got clear of the heavy overhead growth and around to the back of the rock shelf. Just before the fabric and sticks flared out I saw that I had an eay climb up to the plane.

I used the Zippo again, flicking it on and off when I needed illumination. The rock was dry and solid and the vines growing over it gave me good handholds. I pulled myself up, ribs aching, breath short, until I reached the rear door, which had been buckled and almost torn out by the impact of the crash. I didn't want to be back there again, but the way things had gone there were worse places to be. I stumbled around in the dark until I located the bodies. They were cold and stiff and the clothing was soaked with blood. I flicked the lighter, searching the faces and uniforms. It was one of the hardest things I've ever done in my life. I felt like a body-snatcher and I wanted to apologise to the poor bastards whose war had been ended by thunder and lightning.

After a while I found Major Smith of Washington. His head was at an odd angle but he was otherwise undamaged. An easy death for him, which is what you'd expect for a Pentagon man. From body-snatcher I'd graduated to grave-robber. I searched through the major's pockets, ignoring his hip flask and cigarette case for the moment. My hand closed around the cold butt of an automatic pistol. I took it out and checked the action and magazine, identifying it in the dark. Firearms I've always been good with, and the

Colt .45, type B model, with its thumb safety-catch, additional grip safety and manual cocking, was as familiar to me as, well, you can guess what I had in mind. The Colt was fully loaded and I noticed something I'd experienced before—a pistol warms up very quickly in your hand.

I moved through the plane. A little starlight was shining through the gaping hole which had been my exit hatch. I located the coats and blankets I'd thrown over the raw metal when I'd quit the plane. The smell of leaked fuel was stronger over here and I judged that whatever force it was that had looked after me all these years had been working overtime that night. The fuel tank had somehow been protected from the sparks that fly when metal scrapes on rock and wires carrying electric current short out.

I heard a scrambling noise, muttered Japanese curses and the sound of over-taxed lungs gasping for breath. Harry's head appeared over the rock ledge. His glasses flashed in the moonlight. His fingers, cut and bleeding, clung to the edge. I pointed the .45 at his right lens.

I clicked the lighter and held the small flame aloft so he could see the way things were. 'Come on up, Harry,' I said. 'We got some fat to chew.'

CHAPTER THREE

'I'm all tuckered out, buddy. Give me a hand up here.'

'Screw you,' I said. 'Use your bayonet to give yourself some leverage. Better still, let me hear you toss it back down the rock.'

'I let go here, I'll break something.'

I worked the Zippo. Harry's fingers gripped the rock ledge, but the knuckles weren't turning white and the cuts weren't bleeding all that much.

'You're lying, Harry. You've got your feet planted solid. Unbuckle!'

One battered hand withdrew; the bayonet sheath clattered as it fell. Harry heaved himself over the ledge and lay panting just below the hole in the fuselage. He gasped a few times, spat and got a grip on the flashlight which he'd tied to his belt. The beam would have hit me in the eyes if I hadn't shaded them with my hand.

'Douse it,' I said. 'Or put it on dim. I'm sitting up here on top of the Hershey bars with a forty-five in my hand. Show a little respect.'

The beam dimmed. Harry got to his feet, teetering on the edge of the shelf. 'How'm I going to get up there?'

I cocked the Colt. The sound was loud in the still night. 'You're not, unless you agree, here and now, once and for all, to call this World War Three.'

'The fuck you mean, man?'

'I mean us against them, Harry. Us against them.'

By this time the night was running down and we had to be well on our way before dawn. I tucked the .45 in my belt and helped Harry up onto the wing. We went through the plane like mice in a cheese factory, nibbling at this and that. Our first collection weighed us down so heavily we had to start again, jettisoning most of the loot. We ended up with K-rations, canteens of distilled water, a compass, binoculars, two cartons of cigarettes, matches and two bottles of scotch each. Harry took a few items of clothing and a pair of boots off one of the dead airmen. I couldn't begrudge him, his feet had a lot of work ahead of them.

I located my kitbag where I'd stowed it under my seat. It was easy to find because the seat wasn't there any more. I took out my shaving tackle and some other odds and ends. The uniform I was to wear in Australia, the brigadier-general togs, were neatly folded. My US uniform was a muddied, bloodied mess so I changed. Harry watched me impassively.

'How old're you, Dick?'

'Me? Thirty—'

'The hell you are. That grey hair on your chest makes you forty plus.'

Lucky he didn't know how much dye I had in my hair. I slipped on the jacket. Good fit. 'What's it matter?'

'I just like to know all I can about who I'm teamed up with.'

I ignored that. 'We'd better get their money,' I said. 'A few quid could come in handy.'

'You're talking funny.'

'Australian,' I said. 'In this get-up, I feel like one again.'

It was a nasty job but we emptied all the wallets we could find and ended up with six or seven hundred dollars. We divided it fifty-fifty, neither of us liking what we were doing. Harry removed a briefcase from under the corpse of Major Smith. He opened it and took out a pearl-handled revolver. He stood with the flashlight in one hand and the gun in the other. I had money in both hands. We looked at each other.

'Us against them,' Harry said. He stuffed the gun into the webbing pack he'd collected things in and slung the pack over his shoulder. I acted unconcerned and took a look inside the briefcase. It contained several letters in long, official-looking envelopes. I put them in my pocket and fastened my own pack.

'You know what we have to do next, Dick, don't you?'

'Piss off quick.'

'Uh uh. We have to burn this sucker.'

'Jesus, why?'

'If my fuckin' comrades in arms find this plane they'll get boots and food and ammunition. Then they'll come after us. I figure the other parties that set out didn't make it because of poor supplies. We can't take the risk. We've got a chance with anyone we run into, but those guys back there will roll our heads like dice.'

I couldn't argue with that. I told myself that it made no difference to the dead men and that it was only through Browning's luck that they hadn't been burnt up already. We opened a couple of bottles of paraffin oil and doused the inside of the plane with it. Harry jumped down and put the best part of a bottle around where the fuel tanks ought to be. Then he laid a trail down the rock the way I'd come up. He rejoined me and shouldered his pack. I was just strapping mine on when I spotted the medical chest. Harry nodded. I opened it, took out some quinine, salves and bandages, and we carried the chest with us down the rock.

Harry's hand was steady as he lit a match and dropped it into the paraffin. The fire raced up the rock and we backed away into the jungle. For a second or two I thought something had gone wrong and then daylight dawned with a noise like an artillery barrage. Heat waves surged towards us; the leaves shrivelled on the trees and we buried our heads in the dirt. When I looked up it seemed that a mountain was on fire; flames leaped fifty feet in the air and the ammunition in the plane exploded in a series of rippling cracks.

'Jesus,' I said. 'I could've been in the middle of that.' I was staring at the blaze, unable to turn away.

Harry pulled at my arm. 'With a bit of luck they'll think you were. Better hope so. Otherwise, that crazy bastard Okano's likely to call for volunteers to go after us.'

'You said—'

'Just scouting the possibilities. Let's get moving.'

We set off into the jungle with no particular direction in mind. Our method was simply to make progress by getting through the undergrowth the best way we could. Harry used his bayonet, which he'd recovered from where it had fallen, to slash away at vines and creepers. I could hear his breath rasping after thirty minutes but I didn't volunteer to take over. I was exhausted, moving like a robot and, anyway, he was doing a great job, his old field worker skills coming right back to him. I was conscious of only one thing—we were going downhill. I don't think I could've taken more than ten steps on an upgrade.

The stars began to pale out as the sky lightened. God knows how, but Harry kept going and I kept following him, more out of fear of being left behind than hope of ever getting out of the jungle. The sun came up quickly and the jungle began to steam around us. I tried to remember what wild animals they had in New Guinea but nothing came back to me from my schooldays. I think the only mention New Guinea ever got was as a place copra came from, and what the hell was copra? My body was drained of all strength and my mind was wandering. I stumbled on, dropping to my knees and crawling after Harry when he decided to go under something rather than round or through it. I could still hear him thwacking away at the bush.

'Now for New Guinea, and a crack at the Japs.' The line delivered by Errol Flynn in one of his potboilers came suddenly into my head as I scrambled through the bush. I was filled with an anger that carried me on for another mile or so—I'd like to have seen that Flynn in the jungle up against my mate, Harry Kaminaga. He wouldn't have lasted ten seconds.[3]

'Fuck you, Flynn,' I shouted.

Harry stopped slashing and turned around to look at me. His entire upper body was drenched in sweat and his face was cut in a hundred places by the thorns and prickles he'd slashed through. His forefinger had slid an inch down the blade of the bayonet beyond the guard and was deeply cut. I could see the white flesh and seeping blood.

'What?' Harry said.

'Nothing.'

He turned back towards the jungle, lifted his arm and collapsed in a heap. I dragged him under the cover of a tree and gave him some water. He barely had the strength to swallow.

'Time for a spell, Harry,' I said.

'How far, would you say?'

'Who knows? Ten miles?'

'Oughta be enough.'

I took a chocolate bar from my pack and fed half of it to him, a piece at a time. I ate the rest myself and smoked the greatest cigarette of my life. The distilled water left Dom Perignon for dead.

'I should have taken their dog tags,' I said.

Harry's eyes were fluttering as he drifted towards sleep. 'You what?'

'The dog tags. So their relatives could be notified.'

Harry's face split into a grin. Just for an instant he was the Honolulu pimp again, the smart Jap in the white sharkskin suit. 'You're an optimist, Dick. That's what I like about you. Want to take first watch?'

He was asleep before I could answer.

Who were we kidding? We both slept for three or four hours. My watch had survived the whole ordeal, but it was set to Burbank time. It showed nine a.m. but the sun was too high for that. I made a guess at eleven and reset the watch. Then I nudged Harry. He came awake, muttering in Japanese.

'No savvy, Harry. Collect your thoughts. We're going to have to decide which way to go. I vote east.'

Harry knuckled his eyes. 'What if we're a couple of miles from the west coast of New Guinea?'

I shrugged. 'All civilisation is in the east.'

'My people are from Kyushu.'

'Meaning?'

'The west of Japan.'

'Let's toss for it.' I found a dime in my pocket and spun it.

Harry called. 'Heads.'

The dime fell on the leaves. Tails.

'Fuck it,' Harry said. 'Well, at least give me the dime.'

I handed the coin over. He held it between his thumb and cut forefinger, turned it to catch the light. I think it was at that moment I decided I could trust Harry, all things being equal. A dime meant a hell of a lot to him—he was an American at heart. I took out the compass and we got our bearings. As I was shouldering my pack I looked back in the direction we'd come. Tiredness and stress play tricks on you. For a second I imagined I was back in Australia, out west of the Blue Mountains somewhere, and that I could look at the horizon in any direction I wanted to. Instead I saw a blank grey-green wall of jungle only a few feet away on all sides. A shiver ran through me. I didn't want to die anywhere, but I especially didn't want to die here.

After a few minutes slogging eastwards, with Harry cutting and slashing as before, the terrain changed. We faced a long climb up a muddy hillside, less heavily overgrown than the country we'd come through, but steep and treacherous-looking. Harry put his bayonet away and gave me a grin. 'Still want to go east?'

I got one of the bottles of Johnnie Walker from my pack, ripped off the foil, drew the cork and took a long swig. I put the bottle back, moved past Harry and began to climb. I've always had strong legs—the result of a lot of running away from raided orchards, shops where temptation had got the better of me and my belt-wielding father when I was young. And from horse riding later.

The slope was severe but the trees growing on it had had their roots exposed by heavy rainfall and there were good hand and foot-holds. It was hard, sweaty climbing, but I fell into a rhythm and went up pretty quickly. I could hear Harry behind me making heavy going of it. As luck would have it, the roots were widely spaced, very suitable to a six-footer, not so convenient for a runt like Harry. I beat him to the top by a couple of minutes and had time to have another swig of scotch and get a Camel going before he joined me.

'I thought Japan and Hawaii were full of mountains,' I said. 'You seem to be better on the flat.'

Harry lay on his back gasping for air. 'Those goddamn roots were like a ladder for you. I needed a few more rungs.'

It was only a slight exaggeration to say that we'd climbed out of the jungle. There was still dense forest ahead of us, but the country had definitely changed. The trees were not woven together and interlaced with creeper. The way was still upward but it looked more gentle. When Harry had caught his breath and eaten a chocolate bar, he unshipped the binoculars, took off his specs and gazed back down and to the west. He held the glasses steady and looked for a long time. Then he swore and spat a brown stream of saliva.

'What's wrong?'

He handed me the glasses. I panned them across the scene. I saw the smudge of brown smoke rising from the trees a long, long way back. 'I don't see anything to worry about.'

'How about six Japanese soldiers, maybe seven.'

'Where?'

'What does it matter? Not far back. Let's move out.'

'How much ammo have they got?'

'Not a lot, but some.'

I was tired after my showy climb. I wanted to lie there on the grass, maybe smoke another cigarette, even brew up some coffee. 'They'll never make the climb,' I said. 'Not in the boots they've got and in their condition.'

Harry was restrapping his pack. 'You want to bet your head on that?'

We moved out, united. There's nothing so powerful to a soldier as fear of the army he's deserted. I speak from experience. In 1917 I deserted from the 1st AIF in France and joined up with a British and a German deserter.[4] I've never known a tighter comradeship, and that's how Harry and I were behaving now. He didn't need his bayonet and my long legs weren't any advantage. We moved as one, slogging through what they now call a rainforest.

After a while the truth of that description became dramatically clear. The tree canopy was heavy and I didn't notice the sky darkening overhead as the afternoon wore on. Suddenly thunder was rolling all around us and the rain fell as if a giant fire hydrant had been opened just above our heads. We were instantly soaked and there was no point in looking for shelter. We kept moving. Rain makes me miserable. It reminds me of time I had to spend inside as a kid, under my mother's watchful eye and tormented by my older brother, Tom, who liked to pepper me with questions like, 'Who is the Prime Minister of England?' I could never see why it mattered. Tom was great mates with our cousin, Rory, a favourite of our father. Rory liked to play a game in which he was a boxer and I was a punching bag.

But Harry was whistling and humming. Tuneful he wasn't, but eventually I recognised it—'On the sunny side of the street'.

'What're you so cheerful about?'

'I'm thinking about those assholes behind us. I'm pretty damn sure they couldn't have got to the climb before the rain came.'

I could see what he meant. The rain would've turned that slope into a mudslide, impossible to climb. And if the Japanese had got around and up somehow, they'd have no way of knowing what direction we'd taken.

Tramping along, wet to the skin, I felt relieved enough to sing a few bars:

Grab your coat, an' get your hat,
Leave your worries on the doorstep.
Just direct your feet,
To the sunny side of the . . .

'Jesus, Dick,' Harry said. 'You're no Crosby.'

CHAPTER FOUR

The rain lasted about an hour, and after walking through the steamy heat for the rest of the day we were both dead tired. Harry was for pressing on to the next ridge but I voted against it by dropping my pack under a tree and getting out the Johnnie red. I realised then that Harry was just as unwilling to be alone in this wilderness as I was. We worked on our bottles for a few minutes. The insects were troublesome and I fancied the air had cooled down a good deal.

'We need a fire,' I said. 'To keep off the bugs and stay warm. Might even try to heat some food.'

Harry grunted.

'Feel like scouting about for some wood?'

'No.'

We sat for a while as the light drained out of the sky. Pretty soon it'd be too late to find fuel. My muscles were stiffening and I was beginning to feel every one of those years Harry suspected I had on the clock—damn near fifty. Suddenly we were both on our feet, shouting and waving. Anyone watching us would have thought that we'd gone mad, but we'd seen and heard it together—a plane, passing quite low over us, heading east. It was hopeless, of course, like trying to catch the director's eye in a crowd scene. I'd done that often enough to know the odds against.

We watched the dot recede in the sky.

'Was it one of yours?' I said.

'I was going to ask you the same thing.'

'Maybe it was neither.'

Harry stared at me. 'A civilian plane? Out here?'

I shrugged. 'We don't know where the hell we are. We might be five miles from Port Moresby.' I couldn't resist adding, 'If only we'd had a fire going.'

'Yeah, or if we'd taken a flare gun from the B52 or had a radio or could fly our fuckin' selves.'

I went off to gather wood. When I got back I found that Harry had spread out a groundsheet and was mixing something up in his mess tin. I dropped the wood and searched through my pack for some paper. All I could find were the letters I'd taken from Major Smith's briefcase. I ripped them open, dumped the contents inside the bag and used the envelopes to start the fire. I fed the wood in and we had a good blaze going in a few minutes. Harry heated his mixture and spooned it into himself. I wasn't hungry. I ate a compacted fruit bar and drank some whisky. Coffee was another matter. The K-rations contained packets labelled 'coffee powder', something which neither of us was familiar with.

'Do you heat it with the water, or pour the hot water on it?' Harry asked.

'Search me.'

We adopted the first method and ended up with a thick dark liquid that looked and smelled like coffee but didn't taste like it.

Harry watched me survive a sip, then tried it himself. 'What d'you think of it?'

'Needs whisky,' I said.

I was tired, but I couldn't sleep. The ground was no harder than ground I'd slept on before, the insects no more busy and the company no worse. I'd been in situations just as desperate, like when I'd been shanghaied into the Mexican Revolution by Dwight Springfield and tricked into joining the Canadian Mounties by Henry Connybear.[5] The difference was that those times I'd known what country I was

27

in, what state and town even. There was something very disturbing about not knowing where I was, not within a couple of thousand miles in any direction. I made a pillow out of my pack, turned up the collar of the brigadier's jacket and tried to sleep. I waited for Harry to start snoring. I was sure he'd be a snorer.

I ran through memories of some of the women I'd slept with. Bittersweet memories for the most part, with moments of ecstasy and despair about equally mixed. This was a getting-to-sleep technique that usually worked. Sleep was so much better than those fights and betrayals, those deceptions and desertions. It didn't work. I was on the point of sitting up to smoke a cigarette when Harry's quiet voice cut through the humming, crackling noises of the night.

'Lie real still, Dick. Don't move a muscle.'

I immediately wanted to jump ten feet in the air. I said, 'Harry. What—'

The pistol shot was like an electric shock. I felt it run through me rather than heard it, and I went rigid, cramping all down the right side.

'It's OK,' Harry said. 'Just a snake.'

I never liked snakes. Tom, my brother, used to bring brown snakes into the house and put them in my bed. I never liked Tom either. I couldn't move. Harry put the gun down and fossicked around until he found a stick. He reached over and I heard the stick make contact with something smooth. Harry lifted the snake up and held it over the fire. His shot had turned its broad, dark head into a bloody pulp. The body, about four feet long, was still twitching. Slowly, my muscles relaxed and the cramp gave way.

'Where . . . where was it?'

'Coming down the tree behind you. Looked like it was taking a fancy to the back of your neck.'

'Great shot,' I said. 'Thanks.'

'You're welcome.' He retracted the stick and examined the snake closely. 'Makes me wish I'd paid more attention in school. Might've been able to identify this sucker and know where we are.'

'I never found school learning much use when it came to survival,' I said.

Harry flicked the snake away into the bushes. 'Ain't it the truth. Tell me how you come to be in US uniform in a US plane and you an Aussie with an Aussie uniform in your kit.'

'It's a long story.'

'I can't sleep. We got all night.'

I started to tell him, all about the Hollywood propaganda movies and John Farrow and the FBI. I threw in May Lin and Bette Davis and Spencer Tracy. He was snoring before I got on to Errol Flynn.

We got moving at first light, wearing our jackets for the first few hours or so against the early morning cold, and then rolling them up and tying them to our packs. The packs were a little lighter for the food and liquor we'd consumed. There was no argument now about which direction to take. We marched towards the rising sun and by mid-morning I was aware that I had a crick in my neck from looking up into the sky for a plane. We went over the first ridge and I caught my breath as we neared the top, hoping for a sight of human habitation. But beyond the ridge was more forest and further ridges. Harry used the binoculars anyway, quartering the field of vision, adjusting the focus. I smoked and rubbed my still-sore ribs. My cuts and abrasions were healing, thanks to the ointments we'd taken from the medical chest. I wondered how the Japs were doing, back in the jungle. Then I forgot about them.

We pushed on and at the first rest stop Harry busied himself by cutting off his sergeant's insignia and turning his jacket inside out. The drab green cloth was a light beige on the inside. He tore the peak from his cap, rubbed mud into it and pulled it out of shape so that it looked like a brown beret.

'What's the idea?'

'I'm thinking about that plane. I'll swear it wasn't military. That means I don't want to look like a Japanese sergeant in these parts.'

'I'll vouch for you,' I said.

'That's big of you, Dick, I appreciate it. But Bren guns don't always listen to phony brigadier generals.'

He had a point. He was betting on us falling into the hands of my side rather than his. Fine. But if it came to the crunch, how was *my* side going to treat *me*?

We spotted a few more planes during the day. They were heading south-east and, by unspoken agreement, we altered our course. The planes were military this time, but flying very high and impossible to identify. The country didn't change much and neither did the weather. It rained in buckets in the afternoon, just as before. Dying of thirst wasn't going to be one of our problems.

Like Harry, I hadn't ever been an attentive student. I'd scraped along for a few years at Dudleigh Grammar by a combination of cheating and learning things off by heart, parrot fashion. That kind of knowledge doesn't stick. The result was that although I recognised some of the trees, eucalypts, acacias and such, for all I knew they grew everywhere from Malaya to Tasmania. I'd certainly seen gum trees in California and South Africa. Same with the birds. There were all kinds, big and small, but I've never known anything about birds and all I could say about these was that some were black, some were white and some were reddish-brown.

We spent the following days in the same way—tramping, getting wet, drying off and sleeping. The ground got harder at night after the whisky ran out. The food was monotonous and getting short. We thought about hunting but didn't see any animals worth

killing and we didn't want to waste our ammunition anyway. There
were berries growing on thorny trees and some of the pulpy plants
looked edible, but we didn't want to take the risk. By the twelfth
or thirteenth day we were hungry and losing condition. There were
fewer planes, but those we saw were still heading south-east.

We struggled up to the top of a ridge and Harry got out the
glasses. He stared for what seemed like hours until I got impatient.

'What can you see? A bar, whorehouse, golf course, what?'

'A river,' Harry said. 'I think.'

'Terrific. We can catch fish with our bare hands.'

'You dope. Rivers flow to the sea, don't you know that? The sea
means ships, towns maybe.'

If I'd ever known, I'd forgotten. I grabbed the glasses and made
adjustments. My vision was better than Harry's but he was more
painstaking. It took me a minute to get the focus right. Then I saw
it, glinting in the distance. 'It loops,' I said.

'So what?'

'It makes these wide loops. If we follow it we'll have to walk ten
miles to make one.'

'You got a better idea?'

I'd once spent a lot of time on a river, far too long in fact, with
a band of Canadian Indians. The trip had been a nightmare, apart
from a little female comfort, but I'd been impressed by how far and
fast you could travel on a river.[6]

'Maybe we could make a raft.'

Harry was wiping his glasses. He replaced them and stared at
me. 'Yeah, I woulda suggested that myself, it's just I didn't notice
you had an axe in your pack.'

'There might be some fallen trees,' I muttered. 'Anyway, a river
is something different. I'm sick to death of this bloody bush.'

We pushed on towards the river.

'A raft,' Harry mumbled. 'Huckleberry fuckin' Finn. Why not
a canoe? Hia-fuckin'-watha.'

'I thought you didn't remember anything from school.'

As we tramped along Harry recited:

By the shore of Gitche Gumee,
By the shining Big-Sea-Water,
Stood the wigwam of Nokomis,
Daughter of the Moon, Nokomis.
Dark behind it rose the forest,
Rose the black and gloomy pine-trees,
Rose the firs with cones upon them;"
Bright before it beat the water,
Beat the shining Big-Sea-Water.

'You hope,' I said.

'That's funny. I didn't think I'd taken any of that crap in. You want to hear some more, Dick?'

'No. Listen to this,

I had written him a letter
Which I had, for want of better
Knowledge, sent to where I met him
Down the Lachlan, years ago . . .'[7]

'English poets are all fags,' Harry said.

CHAPTER FIVE

It was almost dark by the time we got to the river. We made camp, not talking much, and ate what was just about the last of our rations. The powdered coffee had all gone—we'd acquired a taste for it—and the whisky was a memory. I'd have given a lot for a cup of tea, which was a drink I hadn't taken for thirty years. There was something about the air, the sound of the river, the look of the stars, that reminded me of picnics I'd been on in the Hunter Valley as a boy. The adults all drank hot, strong, sweet tea—all except my father, that is. 'Wild Bill' drank beer and rum. Some of that would have gone down well, too, but just then I'd have settled for tea.

I lit a cigarette and leaned back against a tree trunk which I'd checked carefully for resident snakes.

'Didn't see any logs lying around waiting to be made into a raft by any chance, did you, Dick?'

A plane went over, fairly low, but it was too dark to see its markings. I fancied that the numbers of planes had increased, but I was losing interest in them.

'No,' I said. 'The blacks used to get big sheets of bark off the trees and tie the ends to make canoes.'

'Yeah? How'd they stop the water getting in?'

I tried to remember from the school excursion where I'd picked up this bit of information. We'd gone up the Hawkesbury River a distance and seen the scars on the tree trunks. It seemed so long ago, in another lifetime. Browning Minor of the Lower Fourth. God.

'I think they caulked them with mud.'

'Great. How'd they get the bark off the trees?'

'Stone axes?'

'Got one handy?'

I didn't answer. I finished the cigarette and prepared to sleep.

'We're dead men if we don't get help in a couple of days. How're your feet?'

I'd taken my boots off and washed my feet in the river. Blisters had broken, reformed and broken again. I'd tried not to notice the redness around the affected spots. We'd exhausted the ointments. 'Bad,' I said.

'Likewise. I got infected cuts and bites all over me. I think a coupla my teeth are loose. My gums are mushy. You know what that means?'

'Scurvy.'

'Right. Lousy diet, lousy hygiene. Have you looked at yourself the last few days?'

'No.'

'You look like shit.'

I rubbed my face. Although I'd brought shaving tackle I hadn't used it. What was the point? Now I had a beard that was thick, dirty and no doubt partly grey. I've always had fast-growing hair. It was curling over my ears and the grey would be growing through the dye. I'd done no more than splash my face with rain-water for a week. My hands and clothes were filthy. Suddenly, my face felt alive with dirty hair—growing from my nostrils into the shaggy beard, sprouting from my ears. I realised that I must look like a Darlinghurst wino. *Darlinghurst, Sydney. Why did I think of that?*

'You don't exactly look like Crown Prince Akihito yourself.'

Harry spat into the fire. 'Don't talk to me about those bastards.'

'How d'you feel about Hitler?'

'If I had him here I'd hold him under in the fuckin' river until he stopped kicking. Mind you, I'd do the same with Churchill.'

'Right,' I said. 'Maybe we should rest up here for a few days. Try to catch fish. Give our feet a chance to heal. Look for food.'

'Pity we don't have any of those black guys you spoke of around. What happened to them?'

'A lot got wiped out.'

'Same in Japan. They rubbed out the Ainu, people who owned the fuckin' country in the first place. Come to think of it, isn't it kinda strange we haven't come across any people? I mean, the islands I was on were full of niggers.'

'I guess it is strange,' I said drowsily.

'We got a river here. Pretty good country. Rain, good soil. Where're the villages? Where're the plantations? Feels like we're on the fuckin' moon.'

'There's the planes. Got to be people around here somewhere. Just be glad we haven't run into cannibals.'

'There's no meat on me,' Harry said.

I looked down at my own flat belly. Just the thing for beside the pool in Beverly Hills, but worrying out here. I was gripped by a fierce hunger. 'We'll make it,' I said.

Harry snored.

I lay awake for hours, worrying about everything. I decided I could hear crocodiles grunting in the river. I threw more wood on the fire and held a leafy branch ready to use as a fire stick. But the hard push we'd made to the river caught up with me. I stopped hearing things and fell into a deep sleep.

The boot thudded into my ribs in the same spot Harry had hit nearly two weeks before. It was still sore there and I yelped with pain as I came awake out of a dream about tea and scones. The sun was well up and shining directly into my eyes, blinding me.

'Harry,' I said. 'What the hell . . .'

'Get up, Yank,' a drawling Australian voice said. 'And explain your bloody self.'

'I'm not a Yank.'

'Sound like one to me.'

I got to my feet stiffly, with my ribs protesting. The man holding the Lee Enfield a few inches from my chest wore an Australian army uniform with corporals' stripes. He was about my size, but his youth, erect carriage and slouch hat made him seem a lot bigger. I tried to straighten up and my bones cracked. I shot a look to my left. Harry was stretched out on the ground. There was blood on his face. Two privates stood over him with their rifles at the ready.

'Put up a bit of a fight, that Jap,' the corporal said. 'Game little bugger. You slept right through it.'

'We've been walking for a fortnight, Corporal. I was tired.'

I'd been sleeping with my jacket lapels turned up around my ears. As I smoothed them down the badges came into view and the corporal's eyes widened. 'Jesus Christ,' he said. For a second I thought he was going to salute, but the rest of my appearance convinced him not to. 'Who the hell are you?'

'Richard Browning,' I said instinctively. 'That is, Dick Kelly. I mean . . .'

He tucked the rifle muzzle up under my ear and grabbed my dog tags. 'Kelly, R,' he read. 'United States army. What're you doing in an Australian officer's uniform?'

'I can explain.'

'You better.' He retreated a step and the .303 was pointed at my chest again. 'I'm taking you prisoner. Private Clancy!'

'Corporal?'

'Get divvy HQ to send a truck. We've got a couple of prisoners to bring in.'

The private slung his rifle and went across to where a field radio was placed under a tree. I heard him crank the handle and begin putting out a call sign. Harry didn't move. The other private stared at him as if he had three legs.

'What's your name?' I said.

'Corporal Colin Clark. Australian Militia, North Queensland second unit.'

'Militia! Queensland! You mean we're in Australia?'

'Of course we're in bloody Australia.'

'Where are we?'

'About a hundred miles from Cooktown.'

I moved forward to embrace him. He stepped back, brought his rifle butt up sharply and cracked me on the temple. I felt the ground slip away from under me and I thought I heard the call of a kookaburra, but I might have already been unconscious.

I came to my senses in the back of a covered truck jolting along a bush track barely wide enough to take it. The back flap was open, and I could see the tree branches springing back after the truck had flicked them aside. I sat up and my head screamed at me to lie down again. I did and found Harry beside me, still and pale. His sparse beard sprouted in patches and the blood had dried around his right eye, giving him the look of a battered doll. Our packs were on a bench beside Corporal Clark, who had his trusty .303 at the ready.

'Is he dead?' I said.

'Your Jap mate? No, I don't think so. He is your mate, isn't he?'

'In a way.' I slapped my pockets, then remembered that I'd run out of cigarettes the day before. 'Have you got a smoke, Corporal?'

He took out a pouch, rolled a cigarette and lit it with a match. He flicked the match out over the tray and I waited for him to pass the cigarette to me. He continued to draw on it luxuriously. 'Not for Jap lovers, I don't,' he said.

I wouldn't give him the satisfaction of lying down. I struggled up and took a good look as we bowled through a gate into the militia base. Like all such places, it was a cross between a playground and a prison. It was dusty, laid out in a series of grids, and there wasn't a tree within the perimeter. A high wire fence surrounded it and the Australian flag hung limply on a pole in the exact centre of the camp. The pole cast a long, late afternoon shadow. The grey-green bush grew right up to the fence and poked through and over it in some places. You had to wonder what the fence was for. It wouldn't have kept a reasonably agile grandmother in or out.

The truck threw up dust as it came to a skidding stop outside a Nissen hut. The corporal jumped down and began shouting orders. Men arrived at the double and carried Harry into the hut.

'Down, you,' Clark said.

'I'm injured. I need help.'

'I'll help you with my boots.'

Much as I hate to say it, what I did next came straight from Errol Flynn. He had a way of smiling as he spoke and biting the words off to get them across with perfect clarity. I tried it now, although the beard obscured some of the effect. 'You are showing excessive zeal, Corporal Clark. Believe me, you will come to regret it. Now, if that is the sick bay then you've shown good judgment in bringing us here, but I require assistance to reach it. Do you understand?'

Brutes like Clark are all toadies at heart. A touch of their own medicine, dressed up a little, will usually bring them to heel. Clark could feel that he might be heading for trouble here. His instinct was to use the rifle butt and boot but just occasionally his brain came into play. He shouted something incomprehensible and two black men dressed in singlets and shorts came running. They climbed up and favoured me with wide white grins.

'Help this man into the sick bay, you two. And don't drop him. He might break.'

If Clark thought I'd feel demeaned by being handled by black men he was wrong. I'd got used to them in America, and I'd heard Armstrong play and seen Louis fight too often to think they were inferior.

'I've got crook feet,' I said. 'Also feel a bit dizzy. D'you mind giving me a hand?'

'You'll be right, boss.' One of the Aborigines bent and picked me up as if I was a baby.

'Jesus Christ,' I said. 'I know I've lost weight but I must be still around eleven stone. What d'you do for a living?'

'Cut railway sleepers, boss. I can carry one on each shoulder. Charlie, get those packs, and keep your bloody thievin' hands out of them.'

Of course I could have walked, but I was determined to play the injured mystery man part for all it was worth. I was carried into the Nissen hut, which was partitioned into about a dozen open-ended compartments, and placed on a canvas army cot. Harry was lying on a cot in the next stall, still not moving. Charlie put our packs beside me. 'Thanks,' I said. 'Buy you a drink later.'

'Get moving!' Clark was standing in the doorway. 'And get that bloody latrine dug deeper.'

The man who'd carried me shot me a wink before he left the hut. Clark's boots rang on the cement slab floor.

'Those are natives, in case you didn't notice. They are not permitted to consume alcohol.'

'Clark, you're a pain in the bum. Where's the bloody MO?'

Knowing the lingo, and being a military malingerer from way back, helped. Clark still looked as if he'd prefer to boot me in the head a few times rather than answer my questions, but caution was getting the better of him. 'Be along shortly,' he muttered.

Across the aisle from me a few other beds were occupied. The men lay alarmingly still under mosquito nets.

'What's the matter with them?' I asked.

'Combination of fever, booze and bludging.'

I was looking forward to dealing with a higher, and hopefully more sympathetic, power than Corporal Clark. It was very hot in the tent and I was sweating freely. My head ached and my feet were sore. Lying on a clean army blanket brought home to me how dirty I was. Suddenly, I itched everywhere. 'I need a bath.'

'That's probably the first true thing you've said.' Clark chuckled at what he evidently thought was a cutting witticism. Then his metal-tipped boots were clanging on the concrete again and he was snapping a salute.

'At ease, Corporal. You'll damage your spine banging your feet down like that.'

A tall, thin man sauntered into the hut. He wore a khaki shirt with badges of rank, moleskin trousers and a red tie. His officer's cap was worn on the back of his head with the peak well off-centre. He carried a stethoscope in one hand and a lit cigarette in the other. He crossed straight to Harry's cot and I lost sight of him.

'He's a Japanese prisoner of war,' I said loudly. 'My prisoner, actually. He is exhausted, has scurvy and infected wounds and he's been bashed by Corporal Clark and his bully boys, who will be sorry they did so.'

'Shut up!'

I lay back on my cot and did as I was told. I heard vaguely recognisable sounds—clothes being stripped away, boots being removed, Harry's harsh wheezy breath, the click of a cigarette lighter. I drifted into sleep despite my aches and pains. I woke up to the feel of a cool hand on my forehead.

'How's Harry?' I said.

'Your Nipponese companion I take it? Commendable concern for the enemy. He'll be all right. He needs rest and vitamin C. Neither is a priority of the military authorities, however.'

'Who're you?'

'You're sadly out of touch. I'm the conchie doctor. Lieutenant Barrymore Crawford, at your service.'

I closed my eyes. 'No-one in Australia's called Barrymore. Can't happen.'

'Wrong, but that's by the by. Let's take a look at you. Hmm, nasty crack on the head. Clark's work unless I miss my guess. Willy Johnson says he carried you in on account of sore feet. D'you think you could take your boots off? I must say, old chap, you're rather gamey.'

'So would you be, if you'd been out in the bush for two weeks.' I forced myself to sit up and unlace my boots. I kicked them off and let Dr Crawford remove the socks. The process took some skin with it and I groaned.

'Courage, courage. Very nasty. You're going to lose a couple of nails at the very least. No actual toes, I'd say, given a bit of luck.'

'Terrific. Have you got drugs, you know, sulphur powder, whatever?'

'It's easy to see you've been exposed to Americans. We do our best, Australian style.'

'Jesus,' I said. 'I remember Australian style. A few of my aunts and uncles died from it.'

'We've moved on,' Crawford said. 'A little. I think I hear the approach of our leader. Which hand do you salute with, the left or the right? I can never recall.'

'The right,' I said.

Crawford butted his cigarette on the concrete.

'Conformity never interested me.' He stood as an officer entered the hut, and saluted smartly with his left hand. He held the stethoscope in it. The instrument dangled in front of his face.

CHAPTER SIX

The officer was middle-aged, red-faced and wearing a major's pips. 'You're a fool, Crawford.'

'Yes, sir. Very good, sir.'

'If you weren't a good doctor I'd have you digging latrines with the coons.'

'With the who, sir?'

The major turned purple; he raised his swagger stick as if to hit the doctor, but managed to restrain himself. 'The coons, the darkies, the niggers,' he shouted.

'Ah, yes. The native assistants. I remind you, Major Gordon, that I have agreed to perform only medical duties. I regard any other tasks I may perform as optional. I would prefer not to shovel shit, although I suppose such an activity could be construed as medically related if . . .'

Major Gordon ignored the doctor and beckoned to Clark, who was standing stiffly by the door. 'Corporal, who are these men?'

Clark rattled off a few sentences about 'apprehended in an armed condition' and 'belligerent intent' as if he was quoting from some manual. He finished with, 'Seems confused as to his identity and nationality, sir.'

'Both men are suffering from exhaustion and infected lesions,' Crawford said. 'They are therefore—'

He was interrupted by one of the patients on the other side of the hut throwing a fit. He shouted and heaved, tearing down the net and upsetting his cot. Crawford rushed across to restrain him. Clark moved to help him but the major gestured with his stick.

'Stand your ground, Corporal. I'm sure the doctor can cope and, if not, he can summon a couple of his Abo pals. Did you say these men were armed?'

'Yes, sir. The Jap carried a revolver and the other one had a Colt .45 automatic. Both fully loaded.'

'Not quite,' I said. 'One round from the revolver was used to kill a snake. The Jap, as the Corporal calls him, saved my life.'

Gordon's colour had returned to normal, which was several shades lighter than a plum. He looked down at me; from my angle he appeared to have two faces—the original one, small-chinned and piggy-eyed, was encased in a thick layer of fat. He smiled, showing bad teeth. I'll swear I could smell his breath. 'Really?' he said. 'How comradely. I thought a soldier's purpose was to kill the enemy. I have to conclude, from this talk of pistols and snakes, that you and the Jap did not consider yourselves enemies.'

I shook my head. 'We were trying to survive. We called a truce.'

'How interesting. You called the war off while you played games in the bush, did you?'

Clark coughed. 'He was wearing US military identification, sir, and parts of an Australian officer's uniform.'

'Brigadier general, actually,' I said, trying for the Flynn effect again.

It didn't cut any ice with Gordon. Being one, he *knew* that no officer would let himself deteriorate into my condition. 'Inquiry at 2100 hours,' he snapped. 'Cooler for now.'

Crawford had re-joined us. 'I must protest. These men are ill.'

'Patch 'em up then, and do it quickly. But if you think I'm going to leave an enemy alien and a suspected spy to loll about in this hotel suite of yours, *doctor*, you've got another think coming. One hour. See to it, Corporal.'

'Sir!'

Crawford winced as Clark turned and slammed his boots down before making his exit. 'Sorry, old chap. The major is a complete idiot, of course. Voice of a lion, heart of a mouse, that sort of thing. Now, let's see what we can do for you two.'

He busied himself, with the help of an Aboriginal orderly, cleaning and dressing our wounds, sponging us down and getting us both shaved. Harry was still groggy but he managed a few feeble grins when I told him where we were.

'*Banzai*,' he said.

Clark arrived on the hour to the second.

'Prisoners to be conveyed to detention, sir.'

'Very good, Clark. Where are the stretchers?'

'Stretchers, sir?'

'Stretchers. These men cannot walk. Did I or did I not treat you for tinea some weeks back? And did you not take several days sick leave? These men have not had the benefit of showers and clean socks, unlike yourself. If you managed to get putrid rot between your toes, how d'you think they've got on?'

Clark went to the door and bellowed for stretchers. The two Aborigines we'd encountered before, Willy and Charlie, arrived on the double and with the assistance of the orderly and a private soldier, we were carried across the dusty parade ground to a cement block building which had that ugly, straight-up-and-down look all prisons have. I should know, I've been inside enough of them. Crawford strolled along beside my stretcher, flicking at flies with his stethoscope.

'Anything I can do for you?'

'It's a long story.'

'Pity. Gordon has the attention span of a gnat.'

'I was on an American B52 that came down a couple of weeks ago. Trouble is, it was a sort of secret mission.'

'God help you. Anyone else on board of any consequence?'

I groaned. 'A Major Smith, from Washington.'

'Smith. Is that the best you can manage?'

'It's the truth.'

'I'm a bit worried about what might happen when word gets around that there's a Japanese in camp.'

'He's more of an American than a Japanese. He's happy to be out of it.'

'Americans are scarcely more popular. We may be in for a fairly rough time. But chin up, Mr . . . what was the name again?'

I was helpless and in the hands of the Australian military authorities where there were more charges, admittedly very old, against me than against Dillinger. Mentally I ran through the names I'd used in the army—Browning? Hughes? It was hard to remember.[8]

'Kelly.'

'Kelly, if you say so. I'll see what I can do.'

The cement-block prison was simply a series of cells arranged around a tiny exercise yard. The building had an iron roof and each cell had a window placed too high for the prisoner to reach. Good design, because there was no glass in the window; it was just a hole in the wall and a small man might have wriggled through. No hope for me, of course, at six foot two with shoulders to match. Not that I was planning to escape. For all my dislike of being in prison and concern over what attitude the army might adopt towards me, I had no wish to be out in the bush again waiting to become ant food.

The cell doors were made of heavy planks with a one foot square opening at about head height. They were bolted at the top and bottom on the outside, well out of reach of the occupant. The floor of the cell was concrete; the mattress was about as thick as a folded newspaper, and I don't mean the *New York Times*. There was a bucket and a blanket. For some reason, I didn't want to be carried inside. I asked the stretcher bearers to stop, climbed down and walked through the open door. Willy Johnson closed the door and I heard something drop to the floor as he did so. I didn't look at it.

'Clark, where's my pack?'

'Confiscated. I'm putting the Jap two doors away so you won't be able to hold hands.'

'I hope you enjoy fucking your mother.'

'What?'

'You heard me.'

Clark cleared his throat and spat at the opening in the door. I pulled away and the spittle missed me. 'I'll make you sorry you said that. Shove the other one in number six, Johnson, and make it snappy if you don't want to be in number seven yourself.'

Johnson had dropped a twist of paper. I picked it up and found about a quarter ounce of tobacco and a dozen wax matches. The paper was torn from the *Cooktown Courier* of 31 February 1944 and looked recent. I sat on the mattress and listened to the other cell door open and close and the sound of the soldiers' boots departing. The Aborigines moved noiselessly on bare feet. A few voices called from other cells— obscenities, threats to Clark, requests for water, pleas to be released. My need for the tobacco was great but the need for information was greater. I examined the scrap of paper carefully. No possibility of a leisurely read and a smoke; I'd have to read the paper before I smoked it.

The first interesting thing was the date. Assuming the paper was only a few days old, it confirmed that I'd been lost in the jungle for about two weeks. The nearest of kin would have been notified by now. In my case that meant only May Lin, my wife. She wouldn't have shed any tears. Coalminers were threatening to go on strike over the government's plan to scrap their pension scheme. The Americans had liberated Paris. I wished I was there to celebrate with them. I'd had a high old time in Paris after the end of the Kaiser's war and I didn't imagine the booze-up this time would be any different. 'Pig Iron' Bob Menzies and that rat Billy Hughes were celebrating Hughes' fifty years as an MP.[9] Bob Hope had stopped the traffic in Sydney. Again, I felt envious. If I couldn't have Paris I'd settle for Sydney.

Working with care and patience, I tore ten cigarette-sized pieces from the newspaper. I divided the tobacco into ten equal parts and half rolled the cigarettes, leaving them loose and unsealed. Saliva will only hold newspaper down for a short time. Not a shred of tobacco lost. I didn't know how long these smokes would have to last me and, besides, making them slowly and meticulously gave me something to do. When I'd finished I licked the edges of one of the papers and rolled the cigarette tightly. I lit it and sucked the smoke deep. It was rough twist tobacco but it tasted wonderful. I exhaled luxuriously.

'Hey, what about a smoke?'

'Got one for a digger?'

'Give you ten bob for a packet.'

I went to my door opening and looked out. I could see faces at two doors opposite me and the shadow of a hand waving from a door off to one side. I puffed smoke out into the yard.

'Have a heart,' one of the voices said.

'It's twist in newspaper,' I said.

'Who cares? Chuck us one.'

Another voice. 'Don't be a mug all your life, you'd never fuckin' catch it.'

'Got a better idea, shithead?'

'Yeah, when the *coon* brings the tucker he can slip them to us.'

'That's a fuckin' hour away.'

I raised my voice above their quarrelling. 'I haven't said I'll give any of you a smoke. I've only got half a dozen.'

'Half a dozen. Christ! Give you a quid for the lot.'

'You greedy bastard. Don't listen to him, mate. Share and share alike, right?'

'That's communism, you prick. He's a Yank. Think he's going to be in that?

'Shut your arse. Listen, Yank . . .'

'I'm not American. Shut up, the three of you. I *might* give you a smoke in exchange for some information.'

They all fell silent.

'Well?'

'What d'you want to—'

'Shut up, Blue. He's a fuckin' spy. Can't you tell?'

'Les, I'm dyin' for a smoke.'

'You want to get shot for helping a spy?'

'I'm not a spy.' I'd finished the cigarette now, smoked it down to a tiny butt. I flicked the damp, smouldering scrap out into the sunlight. 'And I'm not an American. I'm an Australian, like you.'

Les said, 'I never heard any bloody Australian talk like you.'

Blue was desperate. 'What about Errol fuckin' Flynn? He sounds a bit like this bloke.'

Christ, I thought, *why does that man pursue me wherever I go?* But this was no time to object. 'Right,' I said. 'I've been a long time in the States, but I was born in Newcastle. I'm as Australian as you are.'

The third, as yet unidentified, voice cut in. 'Prove it.'

'Who're you?'

'Jacko Waters. What won the Cup last year?'

I didn't even have to think. 'Dark Felt.'

'What come second?'

'Fair go, Jacko,' Blue said. 'Who remembers what came second?'

'I do. I backed the bastard.'

Everyone laughed. We were getting along fine. It was the first proper social contact I'd had in weeks. A few beers, a good smoke and we'd be slapping each other's backs and playing two-up.

Les was still sceptical. 'Anyone could learn the Cup winners,' he said. 'My brother can recite them from Archer on. Who's the lightweight champ of Australia?'

'Vic Patrick. Welter as well.'

'Come on, Les,' Jacko said. 'That's enough for me.'

'Hang on,' Les said. You could tell that he was the type who enjoyed this sort of thing—a barroom quiz kid. 'Who's the dopiest, most cowardly drongo in Australia today?'

The only current information I had came from that scrap of newspaper. I racked my brains for an answer and it came. 'To my mind,' I said, 'that'd be a toss-up between that little rat, Billy Hughes, and "Pig Iron" Bob Menzies.'

'You'll do me, mate,' Les said.

So we were all mates by the time Charlie came around with our food. Jacko was the least friendly, but at least he managed to be civil to the Aborigine as we organised the distribution of the cigarettes and matches. Charlie got no response when he attempted to rouse Harry.

'What's he doing?' I asked.

'Just sittin' there, boss. He looks orright, but he's not movin'. Doesn't want his tucker.'

'Give it to me,' Les said.

Charlie passed the tin bowl and enamel mug through the opening in Les' door. The meal consisted of a meat stew with a few pieces of onion and potato in it and a mug of tea sweetened with condensed milk and sugar. I'd never tasted better food in my life and I wolfed it down. I wished I'd asked for Harry's portion.

It was six o'clock by my roughly adjusted watch and the light was beginning to fade. Three hours approximately to my hearing. I was starting to feel anxious and I was probably the first to light up an after dinner rollie.[10] We all stood at our doors, puffing the smoke out into the fast cooling air.

'Jesus, that's good.'

'I haven't had a smoke for a week.'

'Better than a tailor-made any day. What's your name, mate?'

'Dick Kelly,' I said. 'Gidday, Les, Jacko, Blue.'

'Gidday, mate.'

'Gidday.'

'How ya goin', Dick?'

Harry's voice cut through the chorus. 'When you've all finished jerkin' each other off, how about telling me where the fuck we are and what's going on?'

'Jesus Christ,' Blue said. 'It's a Jap.'

CHAPTER SEVEN

That put me back to square one with the blokes. There was a long silence, then Les spat his cigarette out into the yard. It lay there, glowing softly and sending up a thin trail of smoke.

'I told you not to talk to the bastard,' Les said. 'A fuckin' Jap lover. Jesus Christ.'

Blue gripped the opening with both hands and rattled the door of his cell. 'If I could only get out I'd be across there and do you and your Jap bastard mate.'

'Go fuck yourself, Aussie,' Harry said. 'Go stick your dick in your fuckin' bucket.'

There was a roar of obscene abuse from Blue and Jacko. Harry taunted them both, calling them gaolbirds and cowards.

'We're not cowards,' Les said.

'No? Why aren't you in New Guinea? Why aren't you fighting?'

'If you yellow bastards come to Australia we'll fight,' Blue said. 'You watch us.'

'You're safe,' Harry jeered. 'No-one's invading your shitty country.'

That set them off into a new frenzy of abuse and door rattling.

'Hey, Dick, old buddy,' Harry yelled. 'Whaddya think of these assholes?'

'Shut up, the lot of you.' I said. 'Harry here's a prisoner of war, but he's more of a Yank than a Jap. Ask him who holds the world featherweight title.'

'Willie Pep,' Harry shouted.

'Wrong, you Jap prick,' Blue bellowed. 'He lost it last June.'

'I ain't seen a paper or heard a radio for nearly a year,' Harry said.

That sobered and silenced everybody. I told the Australians about how I'd met up with Harry and what we'd been through. I told them about Lieutenant Okano and the snake and how Corporal Clark had beaten the shit out of Harry while he was asleep.

'That'd be right,' Les said. 'Clark's an arse-licking turd.'

'How're you feeling now, Harry?' I asked.

'Scared. Am I looking at a firing squad or what?'

The three Australians were stunned. 'You're a prisoner of war,' Les said. 'They'll put you in a camp somewhere. You'll get fed and treated decent.'

'Not like your lot done to our boys in Malaya,' Blue said.

'I don't know what you're talking about,' Harry said quietly. 'But is that the straight goods? A POW camp?'

'Right,' I said.

Harry laughed. 'I feel better, guys. I feel a whole lot better.'

As the light died we exchanged life stories, the way imprisoned men do. In my experience, you can believe about half of what you're told. Les Desmond was a timber worker from southern Queensland who'd refused to go to the war because he was a Communist. War was a capitalist plot. He was prepared to defend Australia if the country was invaded, but that was all. Hence his service in the militia. Blue Richardson had sought exemption on religious grounds. He'd been a member of a pacifist holy-roller sect, but his application for exemption had been rejected and he was gaoled. A few weeks in gaol stripped him off his religion and his application to join the militia got him his release. Jacko Waters had been desperate to fight. He'd volunteered the day war was declared but was rejected on account of his shortness and bad teeth. He'd had the teeth fixed but couldn't add an inch to his height.

'I tried spine-stretching,' he said. 'Hurt like hell and didn't do a bit of bloody good. I wore built-up boots and grew me hair thick on top. No go.'

Eventually, the militia had accepted him. He was working his way north towards the action. The three men were serving a month in the cooler on a variety of charges—insubordination, drunkenness, brawling, destruction of army property and, in Richardson's case, being AWOL.

'What's the drum on Major Gordon?' I asked.

Jacko hawked and spat. 'That's about what he's worth. Fat bugger struts about giving orders, then pisses off to Brisbane every chance he gets. Captain Talbot and Sergeant Rutherford really run the place.'

This sounded promising. 'Where're they now?'

'Talbot's away on a course,' Les said. 'The sarge should be around. Didn't you see him?'

'No. Just Gordon and the MO.'

'Crawford's all right,' Jacko said. 'Funny bugger with that red tie and all. Reckon he's one of your mob, Les? A Commo? Has he given you the secret handshake?'

'There's no secret handshake, you ignorant bugger. No, Crawford's a member of the bourgeoisie. But he wouldn't be the first I'd put up against a wall.'

'Don't talk like that,' Harry wailed.

'You'll be all right, Jap,' Jacko said. 'You'll be back in the paddy fields before you know it.'

'I've never seen a fuckin' paddy field in my life. I'm from Honolulu.'

'Fair dinkum?' Richardson said. 'Hula girls and all that?'

'All that,' Harry sighed. 'You bet.'

'Have they got them in Borneo?' Jacko said. 'I reckon that's where we'll get to fight next. Borneo.'

'You'll never get to fight,' Richardson mocked. 'Less it's in one of them midget submarines the Japs sent into Sydney Harbour. D'ya hear about that, Jap?'

'No,' Harry said. 'And the name's Harry, if you don't mind.'

Richardson spat. 'Fuck you.'

Les said, 'You're a prick, Richardson. Jeez, I wish I had a smoke.'

I could see how the fights would have started and how the property would have got damaged. These men had frustrations boiling inside them with no outlet. But for now they all focused on the problem of getting tobacco smoke into their lungs. It was Les who proposed the solution.

'Dick, if you shove your hand out to the left you can pass the makings to Richardson. He's a long streak of cocky shit, I reckon with a bit of a stretch he can pass them on to Harry. From where he is, Harry should be able to toss them through my peephole.'

'No chance,' Richardson said.

'What?' Les' voice was a snarl.

'I'm not giving anything to a bloody Jap.'

I rolled four cigarettes, kept one and five matches for myself, and wrapped three smokes and three matches in what was left of the newspaper. 'He doesn't smoke,' I said. 'He'll pass them on.'

'That's not the bloody point,' Richardson whined. 'He's a Jap. They're the enemy.'

'Listen, Richardson,' Les said. 'Right now, the enemy for me is any bastard who tries to stop me getting a smoke. Do as I say, or I'll kick the living shit out of you the minute your time's up.'

'All right,' Richardson said, and I could hear the fear in his voice. 'Give us the bloody stuff.'

'Don't you drop it,' Les said. 'Or the same thing goes.'

I flexed my fingers and gripped the folded paper between them. Then I extended my hand through the hole, stretching it as far as I could. With my various injuries and aches it wasn't easy, but I had well-developed survival instincts and Les was the man to be in with in this little group.

'I can't reach it,' Richardson gasped.

'You're not trying, you bugger,' Les grated. 'Shove your shoulder through, it won't bite you.'

I had the beginnings of a cramp, but I persisted and felt the paper gripped at the other end.

'Easy,' Les said. 'Easy.'

'Got it!'

I withdrew my hand and massaged my aching arm. I was longing to light my cigarette but, childishly, I didn't want to finish first. I could hear Richardson unwrapping the paper.

'Righto, Blue,' Les said. 'Other arm out and pass it along to Harry.'

'Why don't I try to lob it across to you? I reckon I could.'

'You couldn't lob a golf ball into a swimming pool at twenty feet. Do it!'

I couldn't see very well, given the angle and the darkness, but I could hear Richardson's gasps again and Harry's quiet chuckle.

'C'mon, Blue, old mate,' Harry said in a dreadful parody of the accent. 'You can fair dinkum it.'

'Shit,' Richardson said. 'Grab it and shut your dirty yellow mouth.'

'*Banzai*,' Harry yelled.

'What's that mean?' Jacko asked.

'Nothing, really,' I said quickly. 'He yells it when he's happy. It means something like "bonzer".'

Les' voice was calm now, the captain-coach inspiring his team. 'OK, Harry. It's not far. Can you see the hole? Jesus, what're you doing?'

'Cleaning my fuckin' glasses, man.'

'Glasses,' Les said.

Harry laughed. 'Might be the time to take up smoking. Got me two good ones here. Just kidding, Lez. What kinda name's that, Lez?'

'Haven't you ever heard of Les Darcy?' Jacko said.

'Less Darcy? Sure I heard of him. Middleweight. Beat Jeff Smith. That how you say it? Lez?'

'Just throw us the makings,' Les said.

'OK. Back up.'

Harry's voice was light and careless. I couldn't see what happened next, but I heard Les yelp.

'You got me in the eye!'

'I told you to back up. I was pitcher for the Nippon Eagles, *very* minor league, but I had a good knuckle ball.'

'What's he talking about?' Richardson said.

'Never mind. I've got the makings. Shit, you've rolled them already. Good job of it, too.'

'I was rolling cigarettes when you were playing marbles.'

Harry chuckled again. 'Yeah, Dick's older'n he looks. He probably knew Less Darcy.'

'Les,' Jacko said.

Jacko pleaded, 'Come on, Les. My turn.'

I could see the next exchange, or attempted exchange. Les stretched his hand out, the paper held in the very tips of his fingers. Jacko's stumpy arm could barely clear the hole. There were several feet of space between them.

'Sorry, Jacko,' Les said. 'It's not going to work.'

Jacko groaned. 'You bastard, Les. You're supposed to be the Commo, and look at what's happened. You've ended up with two smokes.'

Harry's laugh bubbled out above the sound of the night birds and the wind in the trees around the perimeter of the camp. 'Haven't you guys heard about the way things are in Russia? The

Communist bigwigs have got everything and the ordinary people have got nothing. That's the way things are. You can't change it.'

'Bullshit,' Les said.

Harry laughed again. 'Light up, enjoy your smoke. Tough luck, Jacko. Maybe us short guys should stick together.'

Three matches flared and three smokers began to soil their lungs.

Richardson was still in a complaining mood, although he'd drawn some comfort from Jacko's distress. 'Jeez, this is rough baccy. Where'd you get it?'

'From Willy Johnson,' I said.

'Hope he didn't wipe his arse with the paper first.'

'What's the time, Dick?' Harry asked.

'Getting close to 2100.'

'Shit, I'm scared. What's a trial like in this man's army?'

'It's not a trial,' Les said. 'It's a hearing.'

'What's that?'

Jacko laughed. 'They talk and you hear them.'

'That's what I figured.'

I finished my cigarette, which I'd smoked down to the last, finger-scorching, quarter inch. I was feeling butterflies in the stomach and the evening meal was threatening to come up. Tribunals, hearings, interrogations, whatever you like to call them, always affect me this way. My own, that is. Like most people, I quite enjoy a good murder trial when someone else's arse is on the line. When it's you in the dock, it's a different matter. All that interesting legal paraphernalia just feels like a rope tightening around your neck. The waiting is the worst part. You wonder how badly things can go against you and you start to feel guilty even if you're innocent. If you're guilty, you feel more guilty, and start to act accordingly. I'd been called a spy and it was wartime. You didn't have to know much history to realise the potential danger in that situation.

As I stood there looking out into the yard, I tried to think who there might be in Australia to vouch for me. My parents had to be dead or senile by now. I couldn't imagine 'Wild Bill' still being alive at ninety-something, the way he drank, smoked and ate. My sisters were probably married to bank managers or clergymen and living in Melbourne or Adelaide. I'd heard that my brother Tom had died of drink some years back but there was always Rory, my cousin, the tormentor of my youth. I wondered if he'd changed, grown more familial? I doubted it. Odds were he'd inherited the biggest whack of whatever 'Wild Bill' had left and would swear on a stack of bibles I wasn't his kin. No hope in that quarter; the Brownings have never been close.

I hadn't told the gaolbirds much of my own story, but I did now, to check how it would be received by an Australian audience. There was a sceptical silence.

'Never heard of any B fuckin' 52 coming down around here,' Jacko said.

'It was miles away,' I said, 'and badly off course.'

Richardson sneered. 'Still, you'd reckon someone would have heard about it. We patrol a pretty big area and we never got no signal. And that yarn about making a film. You don't look like a film star.'

'I'm not,' I said.

'Well, then.'

'It was sort of a secret thing.'

Richardson went into a coughing fit that seemed to shake the walls of his cell. 'Tell you what,' he wheezed at last, 'maybe they'll give you a secret trial and a secret hanging. For mine, you're a Jap spy. I reckon they'll do the two of youse.'

Suddenly, the gate to the exercise yard opened and there was a strong light flashing and the sound of military boots on concrete.

Here we go, I thought.

A sergeant in a crisp uniform accompanied by two privates, one of them carrying a hooded tilley lamp, marched up to my door and made a gesture that was very like a salute.

'Mr Kelly, I'm Sergeant Rutherford. I'm here to offer the CO's apologies and to escort you to the officers' mess.'

I heard whistles and catcalls coming from the cells of Les and Jacko.

'You bewdy, sarge. Did you tell old fat guts where to get off?'

'Good on you, Dick. You'll be right with the sarge.'

'Shut up, you lot! Private.'

One of the soldiers unlocked my door and opened it. I strolled out and shook hands with Rutherford. All at once I felt fine. Nothing was hurting.

'This way, Mr Kelly.'

'Just a minute.' I crossed the yard and gave the rest of my supply of cigarettes and matches to Jacko and Les.

'Good on you, mate.'

'Thanks, Dick.'

Rutherford watched impassively.

'What about Sergeant Kaminaga?' I said.

'I beg your pardon.'

I pointed at Harry's cell. 'Sergeant Kaminaga, my . . . er . . . . prisoner. I think he'd like some hot coffee and an extra blanket wouldn't go amiss.'

'I'll see to it,' Rutherford said.

I straightened my jacket and gave a thumbs-up to Les, Jacko and Harry. 'Good luck, chaps,' I said in my best Flynnese.

'Don't overplay it, Dick,' Harry said.

CHAPTER EIGHT

There's nothing like a touch of adversity to make you appreciate the good times. I strolled across to the officers' mess, chatting with Rutherford, who treated me as something like a cross between a colonel and a crooner. I felt raffish and wondered if I looked it. I'd retained a handlebar moustache, but was otherwise clean-shaven. The Aboriginal orderly had hacked off a fair quantity of hair but there was still a good deal left. My clothes were a mess but a good carriage can compensate for that. Put a drink in my hand and I'd be ready to cope with anything.

Dr Crawford was waiting for me at the door to the mess, yet another Nissen hut, along with an officer who accepted Rutherford's smart salute.

'Thank you, Sergeant. Good evening.'

'Goodnight, sir.'

Rutherford and the privates sloped off. Crawford lifted his glass to me. 'Mr Kelly, this is Captain Talbot. He's the CO at present.'

I shook Talbot's hand. He had a grip like Johnny Weissmuller. He was about thirty with a square chin, beaked nose and eyes that had seen it all.

'Welcome, Mr Kelly. Sorry for the misunderstandings. Come in and have a drink.'

Some of the best words in the language, those. I went into the hut, which had asbestos-lined walls, a carpet square and heavily curtained windows. The light bulbs were low wattage and the space was very gloomy.

'We're practising blackout at the moment,' Talbot said. 'There's talk of Japanese air-raids.'

I hadn't heard any such talk from Harry, but I kept my counsel. Talbot introduced me to a young, fair Lieutenant whose name I've forgotten and to Warrant Officer Jim Clive. We shook hands diffidently; Clive was getting used to being treated as an officer, I was wondering how long I'd have to wait for the drink.

'Jim's been on a course,' Talbot said. 'We're confidently expecting to hear news of his pip.'

'I was told *you* were away on a course, Captain.'

'Call me Lindsay. I was. Got back today to find this shemozzle. One look at those letters in your kit straightened things out. Why didn't you tell Gordon about them?'

We'd reached the bar by this time and I had time to think of an answer while drinks were being poured. A private soldier wearing a white jacket over his khaki shirt did the honours with aplomb. Of course, I'd snatched the letters up hastily and had no idea what was in them, but that wouldn't sound right.

'Too exhausted, I suppose.' I lifted my glass. 'Cheers. Besides, I knew it'd all sort out in the end. A few hours in the cooler never hurt anyone, eh, Lindsay?'

'Certainly wouldn't hurt Major Gordon,' Crawford muttered.

'Now, now, Barry,' Talbot said. 'The major can be useful at times.'

The whisky was good and the measure was generous. Talbot produced a tin of twenty Players and left them open for us to help ourselves. He only smoked one or two himself. Crawford smoked his own brand, Senior Service. Nervous Clive and I dipped in pretty frequently. I was starting to relax. 'Where's the major now? Seems only right to have a word with him.'

'Gone to Brisbane,' Clive ventured, blushing as he spoke.

I raised one eyebrow, but let it drop when I remembered Harry's warning. 'How does he get there?'

The other three officers were silent, permitting Clive to answer. 'There's an airfield at Cooktown.'

That was good news. Amiable though the company was, I had no wish to hang around this dusty neck of the woods any longer than necessary. I still had the problem of ferreting out what exactly was said in the letters from Major Smith's briefcase. It wouldn't do to be totally ignorant. The officers had already eaten, which was a pity as I could have managed a steak or two, but the drinks kept coming and we spent a happy couple of hours.

Crawford got sloshed in a gentlemanly way, and revealed his doubts about the sanity of Field Marshall Montgomery and the masculinity of Major Gordon. The lieutenant departed early. Lieutenant-to-be Clive drank and said very little. I gathered that he was from a prominent Melbourne family which had put many obstacles in the way of his joining the army proper.

Talbot was the dominant personality. I swear that it was only after an hour or so that I noticed the stiffness of his left arm. It transpired that he'd fought in Africa and New Guinea and suffered a wound that rendered him unfit for fully active service. Second in command of the North Queensland Militia Unit Number Four was the best post he could secure and he was grateful for it, even if it did mean dealing with incompetents like Major Gordon and slackers like Blue Richardson. He drank freely without seeming to be affected. I had to slow down as I was out of practice and I wanted to pick up anything about my situation that Talbot might let slip.

'So,' he said, 'this business is all rather hush-hush, eh?'

'Mmm.'

'Well, I'm sure it can all be sorted out and we can shoot you down to Sydney. It's those Japs out there in the bush that worry me. I've heard the gist from Barry.'

'Right,' I said. 'Yes.'

'Can't just leave them there. Never know what they might get up to. What about the B52?'

'What about it?'

'Well, there'd be things to collect, surely. Chaps to bury. That sort of thing.'

This is where I made my big mistake. 'I think the Japs blew it up. Sergeant Kaminaga and I saw a big fire and smoke cloud behind us.'

'Odd,' Talbot said. 'Why would they do that?'

I shrugged. 'Might have been an accident.'

He shot me a look that suggested he wasn't buying my story 100 per cent. There were a good number of holes in it. I hadn't explained how Harry and I had come to team up, nor how we'd tried to deprive the Japanese of any chance of following us.

'Anyway,' Talbot said. 'I can fire off a few signals to HQ and get some instructions.'

'Er, when d'you think I might be on my way, Lindsay? And there's the question of Sergeant Kaminaga, of course.'

'No problem about him,' Crawford slurred. 'POW camp in Cowra or some such place. Send him there. Probably make his fortune running an opium den.'

Talbot knocked back his sixth scotch. 'No hurry is there? My understanding is that your film lark is a distraction from a real film about the invasion of you-know-where.'

This was familiar territory. 'Right,' I said. 'So I think I should get on with it.'

Talbot shook his head. 'Might be more important things to do here.'

'But—'

'We'll see what tomorrow brings, shall we? Goodnight gentlemen. Barry will show you to your quarters, Mr Kelly. I trust you'll be comfortable.' There was a look in Talbot's eye I didn't like as he put his glass down and got to his feet. I can usually tell if someone's seen through me and Talbot had. I tried to carry it off with a manly nod and a weary wave of my Players, but I didn't feel confident. He sauntered away with his stiff arm held at a slightly odd angle. Clive said goodnight, which left Crawford and me to have a nightcap while I finished off the cigarettes.

'Good man, Talbot,' Crawford said.

Too bloody good, I thought. 'I can see that.'

Crawford nodded. 'The men like him. Hard but fair. Won't ask anyone to do anything he isn't prepared to do himself. That type.'

I knew that type only too well. The trouble with them is that they're prepared to do the most hellish things themselves and expect others to do likewise.

'His arm . . .'

'Doesn't worry him. I've seen him beat fit men ten years his junior over obstacle courses that would terrify you.'

'What d'you think he has in mind?'

Crawford contemplated the dregs of his drink as if he couldn't understand how the level had got so low. 'No idea, but you can bet it'll be rigorous. Things get very slack around here when Talbot's away. Gordon likes to play the martinet, but the men get away with murder despite Clark's brutality. But Talbot and Rutherford quickly bring them back into line.'

'Good,' I said.

'How was your Japanese companion when you left him?'

'Pretty well, considering.'

'Les Desmond and the rest will all be out tomorrow, peeling potatoes and chopping wood. Talbot doesn't believe in long stretches in the cooler.'

'They'll be glad.'

'I doubt it. I'm talking about a lot of wood and a hell of a lot of potatoes. Well, time to pack it in. We've put you in Major Gordon's quarters for the time being. I'm sure he won't mind.'

I got to my feet, a little unsteadily. 'That sounds fine. I'll just take along a few of these fags, I think.'

In fact, I took the tin, which had three or four cigarettes still in it. I had things to think about and didn't expect to drop straight off to sleep. Crawford signalled to the barman to shut up shop and we lurched out into the warm, moist night air.

Major Gordon's quarters consisted of a small, prefab house with a bedroom, sitting room and kitchen. There was a portable shower and a portable toilet at the back of the building and other comforts such as a radio and a gramophone. Barry, who confided again, drunkenly, that his first name was actually Barrymore, showed me through the place with the aid of a torch. When I mocked the idea of a Japanese air-raid he stiffened.

'Don't be too sure. The Japanese aren't beaten yet.' I made a mental note to be careful—these men might seem to be out in the bush playing soldiers, but to them they were active participants in the war. Crawford departed after telling me that if I left my laundry at the front door, Gordon's orderly would take care of it. I did and then explored the Major's possessions out of curiosity. He had a good liquor supply and a dozen or so silk vests and undershirts. *Well,* I thought, *nothing in that. They say Churchill goes in for the same thing.* I might have considered pouring myself a drink and popping on a record or two, but Gordon's collection was exclusively operatic, which is a form of music that leaves me totally cold—apart from a couple of the popular numbers and I can never remember which operas they come from. I drank several glasses of water to forestall a hangover and went to bed.

I slept well and late. When I awoke the first thing I saw was my pack, neatly placed on a chair in the bedroom. I scrambled up and dug into it. Everything was there except the letters. The sun had been up for a few hours and the water in the shower was almost warm. I stood under it, soaping myself and singing, until it ran out. I spared Harry one guilty thought. With his cuts and bruises a shower would be just the thing, but there was nothing I could do about it and, anyway, an enemy prisoner couldn't expect too much. The prisoner of war camp sounded . . . what was the word? I tried to remember it from my own days in the army. It came to me as I was drying myself on one of the Major's thick towels. Cushy—that was it. The Cowra camp was probably cushy.[11]

A knock came at the front door. I wrapped myself in the towel and answered it. A private soldier presented me with my clothes washed and pressed and told me that Captain Talbot would be pleased to see me in the CO's office at 1100 hours.

'Have I got time for a spot of breakfast?'

'I could do you an egg and toast, sir. Tea or coffee?' Clean clothes, from underpants to jacket, more luxury. I shaved, trimmed the handsome moustache and dressed while hearing and smelling the sizzle of bacon and eggs. It's the only way to fight a war. Half an hour later, with a solid breakfast inside me and feeling very close to tiptop, I strolled across the compound and between the huts following a sign to the admin block. The sun was high over the dark hills that surrounded the camp and the day was getting sticky, but I didn't care. My misgivings of the night before had been replaced by confidence. Pretty soon, I'd be on a plane bound for Sydney and a continuation of the VIP treatment, with a few extra trimmings.

I turned the last corner and saw a group of men standing outside a prefab hut. A sign tacked up to a palm tree read ADMINIS-TRATION. *Hope there's a fan inside,* I thought as I approached. The men were standing to attention. I wondered whether a salute might be in order. I had an inkling that something was wrong when I recognised the men—Corporal Clark, Willy Johnson, Les Desmond, Jacko Waters and Blue Richardson. Only Jacko was smiling.

'Gidday, Dick,' he said.

'Trap shut!' Clark snapped.

'Yes, Corporal.'

'Morning, all,' I said. 'What's up?'

Sergeant Rutherford appeared at the door of the hut. 'Good morning, Mr Kelly. Captain Talbot would like a word with you.'

It was something about his manner rather than the heat of the morning that made sweat break out on my face. I mounted the steps to the hut and found Talbot inside drinking a cup of tea.

'Morning, Kelly. Tea?'

'No, thank you.'

'Good news for a man of action like yourself.'

'Oh?'

'Yes. I've been on the blower to HQ and the word is that there's no hurry on your assignment.' He stood up and crossed to a map pinned to the wall. It showed Cape York peninsula and the Gulf of Carpentaria, Torres Strait and the southern part of New Guinea. Talbot tapped it casually with his teaspoon. 'We're going in after the Japs,' he said.

CHAPTER NINE

What could I do? What could I say? My credibility was on the line. I'd need some kind of endorsement from Talbot if I was going to get the free ride through the fleshpots I was counting on. But the thought of going back into the jungle chilled me. And the idea of trying to bring in that pack of Japanese led by the madman Okano was enough to turn me greyer than I was already. My hair badly needed a touch-up. Talbot was watching me closely, but I hadn't played the game in Hollywood for twenty years for nothing. Looking unconcerned is an essential trick of the trade and I fancied I carried it off as I stared intently at the map.

'Right ho,' I said. 'Maps were never my long suit. Now, Kaminaga and I marched south-east, basically. And we were travelling for damn nearly two weeks. Where d'you calculate we should look?'

As I spoke I began to feel some relief. It would be next to impossible to find the valley where the planes had come down by retracing our steps. A bit of wandering about in the bush would be okay, especially if we were well equipped. There might be a chance to do Corporal Clark a bad turn or two. I began to feel better. I stroked my moustache and looked guilelessly at Talbot. Then I remembered two things—most of the group outside were prisoners and Talbot had a reputation for severe punishments.

'We know where to look,' he said. 'The smoke you mentioned in connection with the B52 was logged by a plane some time back.

Nothing much was thought of it at the time, but the significance has now been picked up.'

I nodded enthusiastically. 'We did see a few planes on our way out. Worried that they might've been Japs. We didn't know where we were, you see.'

'Quite,' Talbot said. He sipped some tea, put the cup and saucer on the desk and picked up a greaseproof pen. He drew a circle on the map in an area that looked a long way from the coast. I found it hard to believe that Harry and I had marched that far. Relief again. Maybe the plane had spotted *another* fire.

'This is definitely the spot. We sent a plane over low this morning. Aircraft wreckage, no doubt about it.'

It was well short of noon and I needed a drink. I felt in my pockets for a cigarette, but I'd smoked them all last night and after my splendid breakfast. The food wasn't sitting quite so comfortably now. I said something along the lines of, 'Did the recce plane spot the Japs?'

Talbot shook his head. 'Jungle's too dense. We have to go in, but we're in luck.'

'How's that?'

He drank the rest of his tea as I resisted the impulse to mop my forehead. When a man like Talbot says he's in luck you can bet that a chap like me is out of that commodity. 'Have you ever heard of the helicopter?' Talbot said.

I had, as a matter of fact. When I'd been flying planes for Howard Hughes,[12] a lot of the pilot talk had been about aircraft that didn't need a runway to take off. A few had messed around with autogiros and other such madcap machines. Some of the craziest of them thought that was the only thing stopping the plane from becoming as popular as the motor car. The mind boggles at the thought of every American teenager having his own plane—the death toll would be enormous. But enthusiasts don't think of things like that. I hadn't kept up my interest in aviation, but I ran into old pilots in California from time to time, and I'd heard that a straight takeoff, rotary blade aircraft was on the way. I began to tell Talbot something about this interesting bit of history of mine, but he cut me off.

'Yes, yes. Well, as it happens, the army has a Sikorsky XR-4 they want to try out.'

'The army? The air force, surely?'

Talbot shook his head. 'The Americans insist it's for army use only. Something to do with patents, American politics, contracts, rivalry between the services, you know the way they are.'

What he was leading up to was beginning to dawn on me and it didn't make me feel any better. Ordinary aircraft are bad enough. I'd flown all kinds, though never as a solo pilot, my nerve wasn't up to that, and I knew how dangerous they were. Exhilarating, yes, but death machines in fact. Nothing I'd heard led me to think that these helicopter things would be any different and, since they were still in the experimental stage, they were probably worse. I wanted to get something of this across to Talbot but he was in no mood to listen. He sat at his desk and started scribbling. Without looking up he said, 'The party will consist of myself, Rutherford, Clark, Johnson, Desmond, Waters, Richardson and you.'

'Who's going to fly the bloody thing?'

Now he looked up, and sharply. I realised I'd sounded afraid. I smiled at him. 'I mean, I've flown fixed-wing aircraft, lots of 'em, but these new things . . . Don't know one end from the other. Not that it matters because they take off straight up, I understand.'

I was babbling. Talbot looked at me coolly. 'The Americans are supplying a pilot.'

'Good show. Don't they need a clearing or something to put down in? Pretty rugged country out there.'

Talbot was writing again. 'I'm sure we'll be able to find a clearing or two. Might have a bit of hiking to do. Anyway, I'm told these things can hover.'

'Hover?'

He held his left hand out above the desk; damaged arm or not, the hand was perfectly steady. 'Yes, like so. Then chaps can go up and down on rope ladders.'

I couldn't afford to enter any more protests and to fake a bout of malaria, which was the only stratagem I could think of, wouldn't wash. I was stuck. Talbot was desperate for action, like Jacko Waters. Rutherford was a machine, to Willy Johnson it would be a picnic. That left me, Clark and Richardson as the possible cowards. As I've found so often, I'm more afraid of being *thought* a coward than of doing brave things. Just. Talbot held out his cigarette case and I took one, forcing my hand to stay steady as I tapped it on my thumbnail. I leaned down for the light and puffed airily. 'Right,' I said. When're we off?'

To this day I don't know how a virtual prototype of a US army helicopter came to be put into service by a unit of the Australian militia, and the whole deal organised so quickly. I can only assume the powers-that-be had the idea in mind beforehand and were simply waiting for the right occasion. From their point of view, this was it. What was needed was speed of delivery into and retrieval from an inaccessible area of a small number of men, which is what helicopters have been so successful at ever since. I paid scant attention as Talbot took Rutherford, Clark and myself through the details. I tried to comfort myself with one thought: *It'd be worse to have to parachute in.*

The briefing over, there was nothing left for me to do. Clark was to organise our kits and rations; Rutherford was in charge of ordnance; Talbot was in control of communications. I found myself out under the palm tree with my erstwhile fellow prisoners, who had been given the curtest of outlines of the enterprise by Rutherford.

'Why you three?' I asked, accepting a cigarette from Les Desmond.

'We were given the option of volunteering or doing another month in the cooler,' Les drawled. 'Me 'n Jacko jumped at it. Blue's not so keen but he didn't fancy being left there with the Jap.'

'How *is* Harry?'

Willy Johnson had strolled up. Les gave him a smoke and he nodded his thanks as he lit up. 'Harry's doin' OK,' he said. 'He's tryin' to get up a poker game with some of me mates. Those blokes are buggers for the cards.'

'He'll clean them out,' I said. 'He's lived by his wits in Honolulu. He can probably deal four aces any time he likes.'

'Might get a surprise,' Willy grunted. He sucked on his cigarette. 'I seen the helicopter.'

Everyone fired questions at him, even Richardson. In his apprehension and fear he forgot his dislike of Aborigines. Johnson drew a rapid sketch of the helicopter in the dust, working with a twig. The drawing was amazingly clear and precise.

'Doors here 'n here,' he said. 'Propeller here an' rotor on top.'

'What?' Jacko said.

Willy did another lightning sketch of the rotor blades. To scale, probably.

'Shit a brick,' Richardson moaned. 'How high does this thing go?'

Les grinned and pointed to the hills. 'Has to clear them, Blue. I doubt if it goes up into the clouds.'

Richardson's face, already pallid from his time in the cooler, went paler. He shook his head and squatted down under the tree.

'He'll be off again,' Jacko said. 'Best to let him go. Me, I'm looking forward to it. D'you reckon the Japs'll fight, Dick?'

I thought back to what I'd seen of the Japanese—their broken boots, haggard faces with feverish eyes and their diet of sago. I tried to remember what Harry had told me of their ammunition supplies. Low, surely. I was about to dampen Jacko's hopes when I remembered the bright bayonets and the fanaticism of Lieutenant Okano.

'If they're still alive,' I said, 'they'll fight.'

'Whoopee!' Jacko yelled. He pulled off his slouch hat and threw it in the air. He punched Willy on the arm; Willy aimed a kick at the hat and they fell into an impromptu game of keepings-off.[13]

I was suddenly conscious of Les' steady grey eyes trained on me. 'You were in the first one, weren't you, Dick?'

I nodded. 'In France. Towards the end of it.'

'What was it like?'

'Bloody awful. Excuse me, Les, I'm off to have a word with Harry. Who do I have to see?'

Les grinned. 'You're togged out like a fuckin' general. I reckon if you just wander up there they'll let you in. WO Clive might be in charge, I dunno.'

'I met him. On the way to his first pip, isn't he?'

Les spat in the dust. 'Sorry, Dick, but that's what I think of officers. Up the revolution, down with the ruling class.'

Les was about five foot ten and would've weighed no more than eleven stone. He looked as tough as teak and he had the hands of a man who could handle an axe and a rifle as if they had been thrown into his cradle. I definitely wanted him by my side when we went into the valley.

'I'm not sure that I don't agree with you, mate,' I said.

WO Clive was looking seedy. 'I'm not used to drinking,' he said.

He'd hardly had a drop it seemed to me, but some heads are softer than others. I advised a hair of the dog and he shuddered. He made no objection to my seeing Harry. I found him in the exercise yard, exercising. He was doing knee-bends and stretches and other movements that looked painful. He was stripped to the waist and his torso showed bruises and half-healed scratches. His ribs were sticking through but he was obviously on the way to recovery. He saw me, but continued his exercises for a few minutes. The soldier who'd escorted me clearly found the scene boring. He lounged against the wall, holding his rifle sloppily, and lit a cigarette.

Harry was dripping with sweat by the time he'd finished. He joined me in a patch of shade, mopping himself with a towel.

'Boy, am I glad to see you,' he said.

'Are they treating you all right, Harry?'

'Not bad. The grub's good. We had a few nasty types around this morning who suggested stringing me up, but I talked them out of it.'

I laughed. 'I bet you did. Well, just thought I'd drop in to . . .'

He gripped my arm and I could feel the strength fear was giving him. 'Dick, Dick, I'm in big trouble here.'

'I can't see why. You seem to be coping very well. I'm told you've got a card game going. Pretty soon they'll be shipping you off to Cowra.'

'Have you lost your mind? The word is you're going into the jungle to bring out my unit.'

'That's right.'

'Can't you see what that means? If those guys catch up with me I'm a gone goose.'

'I imagine we'll be away a while. You'll be in Cowra by then.'

'So what? If I go to this Cowra, what's to stop them shipping the others there, too?'

The guard stood on his cigarette butt and checked his watch. I hadn't been aware that there was a time limit on my visit, but maybe Harry was due back in his cell. I could see his problem. As a deserter and collaborator with the enemy, Harry wouldn't last ten seconds if thrown in with other Japanese prisoners.

'I can't see what I can do.'

'You owe me, right? For getting you away. For the snake?'

'Yes, but . . .'

The guard shouldered his rifle and started to move towards us.

Harry saw him coming. 'Listen,' he hissed. 'Just make sure of Okano. I've got a chance with the others, but not with him.'

'I don't follow.'

'Time's up. Back inside,' the guard said.

'Kill the bastard,' Harry whispered. 'You owe me, Dick.'

CHAPTER TEN

I sat in the officers' mess inspecting the kit Corporal Clark had assembled. Groundsheet, camouflage equipment, medicine pack, field glasses, rations, water bottle, compass, digging tool—with the Owen gun and ammunition plus knives and grenades supplied by Rutherford, I thought I might have trouble lifting the gear off the floor, let alone carrying it through the bush.

I glanced out the window as thunder rolled in the north-west. Then the rain began to fall in buckets and I felt a wave of relief. Maybe it would keep up for days and delay our departure. While there's delay there's hope of cancellation.

'Nasty,' I said to Rutherford, who was a man of few words himself.

He worked the action of an Owen gun. 'Won't last.'

Talbot entered the mess, shaking water from his oilskin. His eyes were gleaming and he looked as happy as a lottery winner. 'Good, this,' he said. 'It'll clear the air, make for excellent communications. How are we doing, Sergeant?'

Rutherford straightened up to his full six foot one. 'All set, sir.'

Talbot wore one of those watches covered by a leather flap, the hallmark of a man who always has time and never panics. 'The helicopter's due in an hour.'

'It can't fly in this, surely,' I said.

'This won't last.' Talbot said. Another dangerous sign—an officer and a senior NCO in perfect accord.

They were right, too. The rain fell heavily for half an hour and then the clouds rolled back. We assembled in a corner of the parade ground under a rapidly clearing sky. The routine of the camp went on around us—trucks arrived and departed, a platoon marched out of the gate on a training exercise, a mortar team stripped and reassembled the weapon, watched by a lance corporal with a stopwatch.

'Where's Richardson?' Rutherford demanded of Clark.

'Can't find him, Sergeant.'

'Better off without the bugger,' Jacko muttered.

'Speak up, Private,' snapped Talbot.

'Blue's not much of a fighter, sir,' Jacko said. 'I reckon he'd be more of a hindrance than a help.'

Which was exactly how I was feeling, but I couldn't let it show. Talbot flipped the cover off his watch and scanned the sky. 'I don't want you to get the idea that we're going out to fight,' he said. 'Our job is to locate the Japanese and take them prisoner. I want that understood at the outset.'

Fine by me, of course. Except that I had slightly different instructions from Harry. When I looked at the assembled armaments it was hard to take Talbot's claim at face value, but if that was what he really wanted I had no doubt he'd get his way. My status was uncertain. I tried to adopt a vaguely military stance but I was glad not to have to play the part completely. The soldiers stood at ease: Les and Jacko looked resolute; Clark looked reluctant; Willy Johnson wore shorts and the heavy army boots looked strange at the ends of his skinny dark legs. Lieutenant Dr Barrymore Crawford strolled towards us. Although he'd drunk six times as much as WO Clive the night before, he appeared to be suffering no ill-effects.

'Rather wish I was going with you chaps,' he said.

'Can't spare you, Barry,' Talbot said. 'You're acting CO until Gordon gets back.'

Crawford groaned. 'I know. God help me. At least it's payday tomorrow and I can do a little embezzling. Well, I suppose the names of your next of kin are in the files. Good luck, chaps.'

Corporal Clark shifted uneasily. He had no more stomach for this job than I did. My mind was racing desperately, seeking for some escape or even a reason for delay. I had the double problem of my responsibility to Harry. That gave me an idea.

'You know, Lindsay,' I said. 'It's just occurred to me that even if we find the Japs we won't be able to communicate with them. They don't all speak English like Kaminaga. I wonder if we shouldn't perhaps take him along.'

Talbot smiled. 'Didn't these gaolbirds tell you what the course I took was about, Kelly?'

I shook my head.

'Japanese. I'm not bad at languages. Picked up quite a bit of it. I had a session with Sergeant Kaminaga this morning and he seemed to get my drift.'

'Good, Lindsay. That's a big help.'

Then we heard the helicopter. It came in from the south-east, skimming over the trees and making a hell of a racket. It landed about twenty-five yards from us; the downthrust of its rotors threw up water and mud which spattered us before we could jump back. The pilot switched off and jumped down, ducking low as he went under the spinning blades. From the grin on his face I guessed that this method of disconcerting those awaiting him was one of his favourite tricks. He wore a green flying suit and a helmet with flaps and a visor. He splashed through the mud and extended his hand to Talbot.

'Captain, I'm Lieutenant-Colonel Jerry James.'

Talbot shook the gloved hand. James removed his gloves and shook a Camel from a packet he took from a zipped pocket in his suit. Automatically, he offered them around. I took one and flicked my Zippo. James sucked the smoke deep and surveyed our little group.

'Well, first thing is, the machine won't take you all. Payload's around 1500 pounds. Looks like you got a couple hundred pounds of equipment there. I'm a big guy myself and so're some of you. I'd say there's one man too many.'

Talbot's hooded eyes ran across us. I had little hope that I'd draw the long straw and I was right. 'Clark,' he said, 'fall out.'

Clark saluted smartly and did so.

'Phew,' Jacko whispered. 'I was worried there for a minute.'

'You'll be right, mate,' Les said. 'Runt like you wouldn't make any difference.'

'Quiet,' Rutherford snapped.

Talbot, Rutherford and James conferred and then the sergeant oversaw the loading of our equipment by Willy Johnson and the two privates. I stood around smoking and trying to look nonchalant, although my guts were churning. I didn't like the look of the helicopter one bit. It was something over twenty feet long, sitting up on raked struts. It had a large rotor mounted on top of the cabin and another at the tail. It was painted grey with no markings other than some kind of registration number. It seemed not to have a metal skin like modern choppers, but a fabric covering. The pilot looked out through perspex; the poor unfortunates in the body had no way to see out unless the door was open. It looked small and fragile and it made me feel the same way.

No-one else seemed to share these misgivings. The gear was loaded. Talbot crawled into the front with Jerry James and the rest of us huddled in the narrow, low space at the back. The engine roared into life and the rotors made a noise that immediately deafened me. The helicopter shuddered and then lifted off abruptly, tilting as it climbed. I was thrown against Jacko, who opened his mouth in what I imagined was a whoop of exultation—I couldn't hear a thing. When we'd assumed a level course, Rutherford cautiously slid the door open a few inches. I was pressing my back against a solid strut; I feared leaning against the fabric and falling through, but I took a peek through the door.

The bush was not far below and we were moving pretty fast. I guess the 'copter would have had a top speed of about seventy miles an hour, although the noise and the air currents made it seem faster. There was a wind buffeting us about; the noise of the tail rotor occasionally got lost, and there was a sickening feeling of power being cut off. Jacko and Les were enjoying the ride; Rutherford was expressionless as always; Willy Johnson's eyes were big in his dark face but he gave me a grin and a thumbs-up. I was conscious only of terror and cold. I was wearing a regulation army shirt and sweater. I'd discarded the officers' outfit in line with the thinking that had prevailed on the Somme in 1918—badges of rank attract bullets. I wrapped my arms around my chest and shivered. Rutherford glanced sharply at me.

'I'm cold,' I said.

He nodded and looked away. All right for him, in his fatigues and jacket. The others had a couple of warm layers, too, except Willy in his shorts, singlet and shirt. The cold didn't seem to worry him and I tried to follow his example. It wasn't too hard—I had plenty of other things to worry about.

Rutherford got a map from his pack, unfolded it and began to study its shadings and markings. He clicked his tongue approvingly as we made a sudden ascent, lurching and seeming to slide sideways through the turbulent air. I felt my stomach move and had an intense desire to be sick. I looked at the three inches of open door and decided I'd never achieve the necessary accuracy. The thought of the humiliation overcame the nausea, which subsided as we flew on.

After a couple of hours' flying, Talbot pushed aside the curtain that separated the pilot's cabin from the steerage and beckoned to me. I crawled over equipment and legs, glad to have something to do.

Talbot's mouth moved but I couldn't hear him. I cupped my ear and shook my head. He looked annoyed, but grabbed a notebook and scribbled on it. I read: 'Over area where smoke spotted.

Quarter and report.' I nodded and accepted the field glasses Rutherford handed me. I crawled to the door and slid it a bit further open. The cold air took my breath away but made me feel better. I adjusted the glasses and looked down at the dense growth. Just the sight of it reminded me of the hardships Harry and I had endured and *almost* made me glad to be aloft in this crazy aircraft. I did as Talbot had instructed—divided the field of vision up into quadrants and attempted to examine each in detail. The muddy green-brown landscape all looked the same—featureless and forbidding.

After one long pass, the pilot banked and brought the 'copter down even lower. This time I saw it—the burnt-out wreckage of the B52. It lay like a grey smudge among the dun-coloured bush. The fire had spread over a very limited area. The rock face was bare of vegetation but dark and difficult to distinguish from the air. I made a sign to Rutherford. He crawled to the curtain and communicated with Talbot. I continued to stare down at the wreckage. Only I in the present company had known the men who lay there, burned beyond recognition, victims of the sort of madness that periodically overwhelmed the world.

Rutherford passed me a piece of paper. On it Talbot had written: 'Which direction to the J. camp?'

I shrugged.

Rutherford looked at me threateningly.

I tried to remember the scramble through the bush Harry and I had made during the night. How was I expected to know the direction? All I recalled was that we had moved downhill, more or less. I guessed north and wrote 'uphill and north' on the slip of paper. Rutherford passed the paper forward and I felt the helicopter's immediate response as it lifted and swung away.

Jacko was in a highly excited state. 'What's up, Dick?'

'We're getting close, I think.'

'Whacko.'

'Shut up, Waters,' Rutherford snapped and I wondered then if he was quite as cool as he liked to appear.

Willy Johnson was examining the mechanism of his Owen gun. He smiled at me. The engine noise was suddenly reduced and I could hear Willy's voice. 'Nice gun, boss. What've they got?'

'Rifles,' I said. 'I didn't see anything else. The officer's got a sword.'

'A sword,' Les said. 'Jesus. What for?'

I tapped the side of my neck with a flexed right hand.

Jacko slid a wide-bladed knife from a scabbard attached to his belt.

'Put it away, Waters,' Rutherford said. 'We're not here to play cowboys and Indians.'

'What exactly are we here to do, Sergeant?' I asked.

Rutherford scratched his chin. 'Make contact, persuade them to surrender, guide them out.'

'Where from, Sarge?' Les said, sceptically. 'Up here?'

'We'll see. Do you know this country, Willy?'

The Aborigine stared down at the bush. 'A bit. My mother's people use it.'

I was surprised. 'I didn't see any blacks when I was down there.'

Willy grinned. 'You wouldn't, boss. But I bet they seen you.'

We were very low now, seeming to just skim the tops of the trees. Nothing looked familiar, but how would it? I couldn't remember any particular ground level features except the crashed Japanese bomber, and that had been camouflaged. Come to think of it, the camp had been camouflaged, too, and the clearing wasn't large. *With any luck*, I thought, *we won't find hide or hair of them.*

The helicopter swooped, rose, made low passes, backwards and forwards over a wide area. I started to gain in confidence. The thing had to have a limited fuel supply. The other men looked down intently, Jacko Waters most of all. I was beginning to feel the need for a smoke and a piss when Willy Johnson's long brown arm shot out. His finger jabbed and pointed like a spear.

'There,' he said. 'Camp, down there, an' a crashed plane. See it?'

I couldn't see a thing, but Jacko's triumphant whoop and the helicopter's sudden change of direction told me that I could forget all about a quiet return to base.

CHAPTER ELEVEN

If Willy Johnson hadn't been around, I doubt that anyone would have seen the camp. It was thoroughly and expertly camouflaged. The branch and leaf screens I'd seen during my brief visit were artful constructions. Drawn up over the campfires, canvas shelters and the body of the aeroplane, they almost converted the area back to jungle. Almost. Willy's expert and keen eye had discerned things that weren't right—disturbances of the growth pattern, I guess, shapes and shadows, who knows? But once he'd pointed things out to the soldiers, they claimed to be able to see the camp clear as day.

I tried to share in the good news. 'See any movement?'

Willy said he didn't. Rutherford was in earnest consultation with Talbot and the pilot. We circled over the spot a few times, coming in dangerously low it seemed to me, but Willy continued to shake his head. I'll admit it was interesting to see the country from above. The jungle looked impenetrable, but I knew there were rough tracks through it. The escarpment we'd gone over jutted up away to the south-east. A break in the thick mass of trees a little to the west was probably a river. The pilot took the helicopter up in a stomach-turning lurch, then he swung away sharply and we quickly lost height.

Even Jacko was alarmed at the manoeuvre. 'What's up?'

'Goin' down, boss,' Willy said. 'Clearin' by the creek.'

The helicopter hovered over a flat stretch that was almost an island. A loop of the river had been cut off, and only light bushes and scruffy grass grew there. The downthrust flattened the undergrowth. Presumable satisfied there were no rocks or other hazards, the pilot set us down as softly as a snowflake. He cut the engines but the sound roared in my ears for several seconds. While Talbot consulted with Jerry James, Rutherford assembled us beside the creek.

'Weapon and equipment check,' he snapped.

My most recent military service, in the Canadian army, was only a few years behind me,[14] and I automatically obeyed the order.

'You may not be a brigadier general, Mr Kelly,' Rutherford observed sardonically, 'but you've certainly been a soldier.'

'Worse luck,' I said. I slammed the magazine into the Owen gun and wondered if I'd get a chance to use it on Lieutenant Okano, something I wouldn't have any great objection to doing.

Willy unlaced his boots and kicked them off. He took a bayonet from his pack and handed his Owen gun to Jacko.

'I'll scout for you, Sarge,' he said.

Rutherford nodded. Talbot joined us, shouldering his pack awkwardly on account of his stiff arm. A puff of smoke rose from the helicopter cabin as Jerry James lit up a Camel.

'Tricky situation,' Talbot said. 'The camp might be deserted or it might not. If they are there, they might want to surrender or fight—with luck, the former.'

My sentiments exactly, I thought. Jacko coughed to hide his disagreement.

'We'll go in and see what's what. I won't say don't fire unless you're fired on, but I don't want any itchy trigger fingers. Waters, that means you.'

'Yes, sir.'

'Keep to the rear, Mr Kelly. All right, let's go.'

Willy led the way. He seemed to have an instinct for where the vegetation would offer least resistance and, where it did resist, he used his bayonet in the same way Harry had. Unlike Harry, he didn't tire. We made good progress, but I found the pack heavy and the Owen gun an encumbrance. I found myself falling behind and contemplated losing touch with the party and going back to have a smoke with Jerry. Maybe he'd have some Early Times in a flask and we could sit down and chew the fat. When I looked behind me, the bush seemed to have closed up and I wasn't sure I could retrace our steps. Not positively. I hurried to catch up.

After we'd travelled for about an hour, Willy suddenly disappeared and we halted. It was an eerie feeling to be standing, bunched up with the other men, not sure in what direction to look, wondering if a Jap had me in his sights. Jacko nursed his Owen gun like a baby. Les was breathing heavily and I realised that he wasn't as fit as he looked. Rutherford stood as still as a tree; Talbot looked relaxed, although he flexed his bad arm a few times. My heart was pounding in my chest and sweat saturated my clothing.

'Where's that bloody Abo gone?' Jacko muttered.

Willy materialised from the bush on our left. 'All dead, Captain,' he said.

I suppressed the sigh of relief.

'How many, Johnson?' Talbot said.

'Seen about twenty. Could be more. But nothin's happened around there for a good while.'

Talbot turned to me. 'What was their strength, Kelly?'

'Twenty sounds about right. Did you see the officer, Willy? Spick and span type with a clean uniform and polished boots.'

Willy nodded and drew his clenched fist across his midriff. 'Not so flash now, boss. He's spilled his own guts from the look of it.'

'Harakiri,' Talbot said. 'Well, we'd better go and take a look. It appears you'll need your camera rather than your gun, Sergeant.'

'That's all right with me, sir. I've seen all the jungle fighting I ever want to see.' A long speech for Rutherford.

Jacko was disappointed. He returned the second Owen gun to Willy and his shoulders slumped as we pushed through the bushes. Five minutes later we stood at the edge of the camp. I'd only seen it at night and nothing was familiar at first. Then I saw the plane and the place where Harry and I had made our plans. The jungle had started to encroach on the canvas and brush shelters. Pretty soon, the camp would be swallowed up by creepers, grass and trees. Small bushes were already sprouting around the places where the fires had been.

The first body I saw was lying on its back behind a large rock. The head was mostly blown away and the ants were completing the job. I vomited at the sight and heard Les retching as he lifted the screen away from another body.

Jacko spat. Willy Johnson stood back, looking away into the far distance.

Rutherford crouched down close to the corpses, calmly photographing shattered skulls and empty eye sockets. One was enough for me; the body looked tiny and frail and the soldier had carefully folded his spectacles and placed them on the ground before blowing his brains out.

'Better collect the identity discs,' Talbot said.

Rutherford nodded. 'Waters, got a job for you with that knife.'

'Right, Sarge.'

Jacko was approaching the makeshift tent lieutenant Okano had rigged up for himself. I wandered over there, remembering the touch of the blade on the back of my neck and trying to calculate how many of the supposed nine lives I'd already lost. I caught up with Jacko and together we looked at the corpse of the lieutenant. He'd apparently been kneeling when he'd ripped his belly open. A long-bladed knife lay near his outstretched hand. The metal was brown, either with rust or blood, or both. The body was folded forward, the head touching the ground in a final bow.

'Jesus Christ,' Jacko said, 'why would a bloke do that?'

Talbot was behind us. 'Honour,' he said.

Jacko took a step forward and pointed. 'Look, Dick, that must be the bloody sword he was going to lop you with.'

The handle of the sword, ivory-inlaid, protruded from the cushion on which Okano had knelt to deliver his death stroke. Jacko reached for it.

'Don't touch it!' Talbot yelled.

He was too late. Jacko tugged and the explosion blew him from his feet. Instinctively, I hit the ground, covering my head with my arms, and Jacko landed on top of me. I felt the blood running from him, trickling down my neck. Then Talbot was pulling him off me. I blacked out for a few seconds and when I came round I saw Jacko lying on the ground beside me. I rolled away and started to yell.

'Easy, boss, easy.' Willy Johnson held me in his sleeper-carrying grip. I shook and clenched my teeth into my lower lip to stop myself from screaming.

'Booby-trap grenade,' Rutherford said. 'Poor bastard.'

Les gave me a cigarette and he lit one for himself. 'Fuckin' capitalist war,' he snarled. 'Fuckin' plutocratic—'

'Shut your Commie mouth,' Rutherford said.

'Make me, you prick.' Les jumped up and reached for his Owen gun.

Talbot's voice was like a whip-crack. 'Shut up, both of you! Are you all right, Kelly?'

I got slowly to my feet and checked myself over. The force of the explosion had been totally absorbed by Jacko. I was uninjured. I forced myself to look at Jacko. His chest had been blown open and the pink and grey tissue oozed from the shattered mass of meat and bone. Les Desmond took two steps and kicked the stiff, bowing figure of the Japanese lieutenant. The body toppled sideways and lay in the dirt like a broken toy.

Talbot's voice was calm. 'We'll bury the Japanese and take Waters back with us. When you finish photographing Sergeant, appoint a burial detail. I'm going to look around for documents and such.'

'Yes, sir,' Rutherford said. He photographed the dead Japanese and his victim. Then he looked at Willy and Les. 'Get ready to dig, but be careful with the bodies. There might be more booby-traps.'

'I don't think so,' I said. 'Lieutenant Okano thought he was something special. I'll do some digging, too, Sergeant.'

It wasn't that I liked hard, physical work in the sun—I don't. But I needed to do something to take my mind off what had happened. It could just as easily have been me who reached for the sword. Everyone likes a good souvenir. I stripped off and got to work with my shovel alongside Les and Willy. Rutherford collected the identity discs. Talbot emerged from Okano's tent with some books and papers which he proceeded to examine. I dug and shovelled until my back ached, then I dug some more. Luckily the earth wasn't very hard, although it was bound by stringy grass and there were sizeable rocks scattered through it. We knocked off for a couple of stiff belts of rum and water, courtesy of Talbot, and then we went back to it.

Rutherford and Talbot transported the bodies as we dug. It couldn't have been a pleasant job and they had to use canvas, branches and lengths of rope to move the remains. We simply rolled them in and covered them with earth, working fast and trying not to look at their faces. We threw their weapons and meagre belongings in with them. It's surprising how modest a hole you need to accommodate sixteen small men.

Rutherford took a photograph, then stepped back. Talbot stood over the grave and said a few words quietly. I assume he was speaking in Japanese.

Willy constructed a stretcher out of two groundsheets and some tree branches. We set off back to the helicopter, taking turns to carry the stretcher. I was so tired after the digging I could barely move, but I stumbled along and did my share. No-one spoke on the return trip. Les Desmond's dirty face was streaked by his tears. I noticed that Rutherford had souvenired Okano's knife. I don't know what happened to the sword.

When we reached the creek Jerry James was standing guard by the helicopter with an M1 carbine in his hands. He lowered it as we approached.

'Say, that's too bad. What happened?'

'He died in action,' Les said.

We loaded Jacko into the helicopter and scrambled up ourselves. Willy had covered him with some calico he had found in Okano's tent. One muddy boot stuck out; the body looked even smaller in death than it had in life. A fly settled on the cloth and Les flicked at it angrily.

'Let's fuckin' go!' he said.

Harry stared at me. 'All dead?'

'Every last one. Mostly suicides. A couple might've starved to death or died of fevers. Okano ripped his belly open.'

'Mad bastard. He's no loss, but there were some good guys in that outfit.'

'Jacko was a good guy, too. Okano rigged up a booby-trap that blew him apart. You're not going to be too popular around here, Harry.'

Harry shrugged. 'What's new? I won too much money today to be popular. Doesn't matter. I hear they're shipping me south in the morning. This fuckin' war, I'm glad to be out of it.'

We shook hands and I promised I'd write to him in the POW camp. He also gave me some names and addresses in Honolulu to write to.

'What's next up for you, Dick?'

'You mean in the long term or tonight?'

'Long term.'

'I don't know.'

'Tonight, then?'

'I'm going to get drunk.'

CHAPTER TWELVE

The room was nothing much; it had a rather low ceiling with plain cornices and a small ceiling rose. It had no bathroom, that was at the end of the hall. Nothing special, but it was important to me because it was in the Metropole Hotel in Sydney and it was the same room I'd occupied in 1916 when I'd met Les Darcy and was about to get my start in the picture business. I'd done a flit after starting a fire in the bathroom and then served a sentence in Long Bay gaol,[15] but that was all a long time ago. I'd paid my debt to society in that particular instance. No-one would remember me and, anyway, I was registered under a different name.

The army had flown me down to Sydney almost immediately after the burial service for Jacko Waters. I'd barely had time to say goodbye to Les, Willy and Harry. I got the distinct impression that the army found me an embarrassment and was happy to be rid of me. No objections from yours truly. I'd been transported to the hotel and told my account would be 'taken care of. Still OK by me. I was told to expect a phone call.

I cleaned up—no signs of a fire in the bathroom: it had only been a few sheets of newspaper and a towel or two after all—opened the bottle of whisky Barry Crawford had slipped me and waited. Two drinks and a couple of cigarettes later the call came. The uniformed flunkey on the reception desk, who'd raised an eyebrow at my dishevelled, semi-military garb and army issue kit bag—informed me that a gentleman was waiting for me in the bar.

'Has the gentleman got a name by any chance?' I asked.

'He simply requested that you come to the bar where he will join you.'

'More know Tom Fool than Tom Fool knows, eh?'

'Precisely, sir.'

I took a look out the window before going down. It doesn't do to jump through hoops for people you don't know. Sydney had changed enormously in the past quarter century. For one thing it was full of motor cars. Stupidly, I'd always thought of it as a horse-drawn town the way it had been when I knew it well. And then there was the bridge. I couldn't see it from the hotel, but I had seen it on the way in and it had made a big impression. I hadn't realised that Australians were capable of such a feat of engineering. The sight of it took away any feelings I might have had about being back among the rubes.

I straightened my clothes and brushed my hair. *Too long and too much grey showing, have to do something about that,* I thought. I pocketed the packet of Senior Service, also a gift from Crawford, and went down to the bar. I admit that I was feeling cautious, if not downright apprehensive. Here I was, without possessions, cash, a passport or any credentials, living in a hotel on army tick that might cut out at any moment. Not for the first time, I cursed the fact that I'd got too drunk and was too hungover to ask for the American documents Lindsay Talbot had found in my bag. All you can do is play the cards you've got, but it's a bit hard when you don't know what they are.

I marched into the bar, head high, shoulders back, and looked around. It was late afternoon, too late for the lunch crowd, too early for the after-work drinkers, and the place was almost empty. A man sitting at the bar must have seen my reflection in the mirror he was facing. He got up and moved towards me with his hand out-stretched. He was a military type, medium tall and sparely built, but not in uniform. His hair was brushed flat to his skull and he wore a clipped moustache. His shoes were highly polished and he sported a fob watch, which was a style that had almost gone out of fashion. He looked to be about my own age, perhaps a fraction older. There was something vaguely familiar about him or perhaps about his tie . . .

'Mr Kelly, I presume?'

'That's right.'

We shook hands. His grip was firm.

'And you are . . .?'

'Forgive me.' His hand shot out and he produced a card like a conjurer. 'Oliver Featherstonhaugh. I know it's been a long, long time, but I recognised you instantly.'

I looked at the card. On it was printed Oliver Featherstonhaugh, MBE, and some letters which meant nothing to me.

'I'm sorry. I have a feeling we've met but I'm afraid I don't . . .'

He smiled, showing expensive-looking false teeth, slightly stained by tobacco. His hand moved up to his neck. 'Surely you recognise the old tie.'

'Jesus Christ,' I said. 'Dudleigh Grammar.'

'Your speech is American, Dick. Understandably. Given that, perhaps I should say something like, "Class of 1912"?'

His American accent was atrocious but it didn't reduce the cold chill that shot through my heart. I remembered him now. 'Oily Feathers' we used to call him, on account of the hair that stuck up on the crown of his head despite his attempts to plaster it down with various kinds of goo. Well, there was still something oily about him, but only in his manner. In appearance he was sleek and self-satisfied. He reminded me a little of George Raft, who was a guy I always tried to stay on the right side of. Make an enemy of Georgie, and you could bet that something unpleasant would happen to you sooner or later.[16]

I grabbed his hand again and wrung it. 'Oliver! How good to see you after all these years. My word, you do look well.'

A slightly pained look crossed his disciplined face. There was something very alarming about his level gaze and the set of his thin mouth. 'You look rather the worse for wear, Dick,' he said. 'But pretty good, considering.'

Considering what? 'Let's have a drink.' I moved towards the bar. 'What're you having?'

'Scotch and soda.'

'Make it two,' I told the barman. 'Doubles.'

The drinks came quickly. 'That'll be five and sixpence, thank you, sir.'

I reached for my wallet, then remembered. 'Er, ah, I understand my bill is being paid by . . .'

The barman cleaned an ashtray with a practised flick and set it in front of Featherstonhaugh. 'Not the bar bill, I'm afraid, sir.'

'Awkward,' I said. 'You see, Oliver, the fact is I . . .'

Featherstonhaugh detached a pound note from his wallet. 'We'll knock that down, I shouldn't wonder. Keep an eye out.'

'Yes, sir.' The barman laid the note on the till and slid the drinks across.

'Let's take a table, Dick, and have a jolly good chinwag.'

He picked his dark Homburg up off the bar and we moved through the bar to a table near the window. I carried the drinks and, although I resented it, I couldn't help admiring the way Featherstonhaugh had put me in the subservient role. When we were seated he took a sip of his drink without offering a salutation.

'Great days at Dudleigh, weren't they?' he said.

In fact they'd been hellish. Every subject except languages, at which I had a bit of a flair, bored the life out of me, and the rugby hearties and fast bowlers always seemed bent on committing at least one manslaughter before their schooldays were over.

I lifted my glass. 'Great days. You were a prefect as I recall.'

'I was, and you were expelled.'

'Well, you know, there was a misunderstanding, and people were rather straitlaced back then.'

'You cheated at cricket. Bet on the other side and contrived to lose a match.'

Bugger this. I thought. *It was a long time ago and the world has torn itself apart twice since. Besides, what was bodyline all about if not cheating?*[17] 'I was learning to live by my wits, Ollie,' I said, 'and I've done pretty well at it since. Chummed up with Errol Flynn and so on.'

'Have you, indeed? Well, according to my information, you've scraped along in the film business, more or less on your uppers. Various problems with the FBI and the immigration authorities and a spell or two in gaol.'

That was true enough, I reflected, as I drank my whisky. Of course, there are two sides to every story, and he hadn't mentioned my military service in Mexico or my stints in the Canadian Mounties and armed forces. Still, perhaps that was for the best. I've never fitted well into large organisations. I flicked my Zippo and lit a Senior Service without offering him one—two could play at this fuck-you-Jack game.

'We can't all lead sheltered lives,' I said. 'You weren't exactly born with a silver spoon in your mouth, Ollie. Scholarship boy if memory serves. How have you been getting along?'

He took out a silver cigarette case, selected one from the upper layer, which appeared to contain a different variety from the lower, and lit it with a monogrammed gold lighter. 'I had a good war,' he said. 'North Africa, picked up a DSO, got on the Staff and toddled along from there.'

I puffed smoke. 'Good for you.'

'Weren't in that show, were you . . . Kelly?'

Easy does it, Dick, I thought, *don't let him needle you.* 'I was in it,' I said. 'I was at Passchendaele, which was a hell of a lot hotter a spot than North Africa, I can tell you.'

He flicked ash onto the floor. He'd hardly touched his drink but I'd almost finished mine. 'I dare say. That's where we encounter what you might call a gap in the records. No sign of your military service in the first show.'

'My parents were opposed. I used another name.'

'Which was?'

I'd had enough of this. I stubbed out my cigarette, lit another and waved to the barman. 'I'd rather not say. What's your game, Oily?'

It just slipped out but the change that came across his face was remarkable. The too-straight teeth were clenched; the bristly moustache twitched violently and a nerve in the right side of his face began to jump. After all these years, he hadn't lived the nickname down. 'The boy is the father of the man', as the saying goes.[18] His knuckles whitened as he clenched the glass. He leaned closer to me and I could smell his hair oil. 'It may interest you to know I hold the rank of colonel in Military Intelligence,' he hissed. 'And believe me, *Mr Kelly*, you are in big trouble.'

It was hard to take him seriously because, suddenly, he was the butt of schoolboy jokes again—old Oily Feathers, the rumpled, plumpish scholarship boy who sucked up to the teachers. The barman brought the drinks and I forced myself to relax as I took a judicious pull on mine.

'I hardly think so, Oliver. I think if you consult with the Americans, you'll find that I'm in good standing with them and with their opposite numbers here.'

'That *was* true, but since your untimely death, I'm afraid all those bets are off.'

'Death? What d'you mean, death? I'm sitting here, aren't I? Drinking at your expense.'

'For the time being. The problem is, you are now an embarrassment. I need hardly say that the ridiculous idea of the film has been scrapped.'

'Why?'

'Have you been following the war news?'

'I've been lost in the bloody jungle. How could I follow the war news?'

'Yes, well, we'll get on to that. Walls have ears and so on, but you don't need to be a military genius to see that it's only a matter of time.'

'For what?'

Featherstonhaugh glanced around before he spoke. The nearest person was twenty feet away. He put his hand up to his face just in case the guy was a lip-reader. 'For MacArthur to fulfil his promise. "I will return." D'you follow me?'

I did. If MacArthur was about to land in the Philippines, the diversionary film was a dead duck. As an old Hollywood hand, used to movie ideas falling over like ninepins, this was only a temporary setback. Image was everything and surely I had the cards to play. I sipped my drink and stroked my moustache, a much more impressive growth than Featherstonhaugh's effort. 'I'm sure I can find something, Oliver. After all, I survived a plane crash, brought out a Japanese prisoner, returned to the scene, saw a brave man die right beside me, that sort of thing.'

'None of that's going to get out.'

'Don't you believe it. A word to one of the scribes in Sydney and . . .'

He smiled. 'Have you ever heard of a 'D notice'?'

'No. What's that?'

'It's an informal agreement between the newspaper editors and the authorities that certain matters, not in the national interest, shouldn't be made public. You don't imagine we want Australians to hear about a company of Japanese soldiers running around loose in Queensland do you?'

'It was hardly a company. More like a platoon, and the poor buggers starved to death and shot themselves.'

'Still, bad for morale. You can't hope for any kudos from your part in that business, Dick. Sorry.'

'What the hell am I going to do?'

I got the distinct impression that this was the moment he had been waiting for. He treated himself to another gasper and took another pull on his drink. 'Bit tricky, isn't it? No passport, no papers, citizenship very much in doubt.'

'I'm an Australian.'

'Really? Well then, no problem. You simply produce a birth certificate—Richard Kelly, born blah blah, eighteen ninety whatever it was, and we'll take it from there.'

'You know very well my name's not Kelly. I can get a birth certificate as Richard Kelly Browning easily enough.'

'Good, and a discharge from the 1st AIF?'

'I told you about that.'

'So you did. What about a tax clearance?'

'I haven't earned any money in this country for twenty-five years.'

'It's not as simple as that, old boy. The government wants a cut of whatever you earned anywhere, especially since you've been such a big star in Hollywood.'

All very distressing. I gulped my drink down and looked around for a refill, but Featherstonhaugh was showing signs of getting ready to leave. 'What do you really want of me?' I asked.

'Revenge, I suppose,' he said casually. 'When your picture came to us via the Americans, I recognised you immediately and volunteered to meet you.'

'Revenge?'

'You and your kind made my life a misery at school.'

'It was a long time ago.'

'It was yesterday!'

'You've done well since.'

'Have I? I've got a boring office job. I live in Ashfield with a dull wife and five brats while you've been charging around the world having fun for thirty years.'

'It hasn't all been fun.'

'No? How many women have you slept with?'

I cast my eyes up to the roof at the pathetic question but he misinterpreted the action.

'See? You can't even count them. My score is one. Now d'you see why I hate you?'

Mad as a snake and dangerous with it. I couldn't think of anything useful to say. 'What about another drink?'

'No. You've done all the drinking at the public expense you're going to do. I'll strike a bargain with you. Clarify the matter of your military service and I'll see about getting you a passport and a tax clearance.'

I couldn't do it. As Hughes, I'd deserted the army and had probably killed a man. I shook my head. 'I'd have to think about that. How long have I got here on the slate?'

He shrugged. 'A day or two, I imagine. I'll give you the same. You've got my card. Give me a ring when you're ready. Meantime, I'll do a bit of checking. I'm intrigued.'

All bad news. He'd recovered his aplomb but that gave me room to play on his vanity. 'Er, Ollie,' I slapped my pockets for emphasis, 'you wouldn't be able to lend me a tenner, would you?'

He produced his pigskin wallet again and took out a five pound note. He dropped it on the table, picked up his hat and left without saying another word.

CHAPTER THIRTEEN

Not an enviable situation. I wandered back to my room in a state of considerable distress, racking my brains to think of someone in Sydney I could turn to for help. There was no-one. I'd never kept in touch with my family and the only news I'd had of them was via solicitors, forwarding documents for signature and advising me of minor legacies or outstanding debts. These letters had gone in the waste paper bin or the fire and I couldn't remember the names of any of the lawyers. My ex-wife lived 500 miles away in Melbourne, and even that was a shade too close.

Featherstonhaugh was wrong when he said I didn't have any papers. True, I had no passport. The Americans had said that could be fixed when I got to Australia. I did, however, have my discharge papers from the Canadian army and a letter from my agent, Bobby Silkstein. I'd got the letter just before leaving Burbank and had shoved it in my bag without reading it. I seldom read Bobby's letters because they were usually about what a great agent he was and what a lousy actor I was. It's a measure of how desperate I was for human contact that I uncrumpled the letter and spread it out on the bedside table. It was getting dark and the room was dim. I turned on a lamp and read:

Dear Dick

I know you won't read this until you're in Australia, you lazy bum, you. But I just wanted you to know that here at the agency we're all real proud of what you are doing. Also, when you get back, you can name your part—Charisse's legs, Russell's tits, Grable's ass. Hah, hah.

Best of luck from all of us working stiffs at Silkstein's Agency to the Stars.

Your pal,

The letter was signed 'Bobby'—the single word took up nearly as much space on the page as the message. No-one ever accused Bobby Silk of being subtle, but there, friendless and alone on the other side of the world, the letter almost brought tears to my eyes.

Get a grip on yourself, Dick, I thought. *You've been in tougher spots than this.* I felt hungry, but I wasn't going to pay the high prices I was sure they'd charge in the hotel. In a strange city there's only one place to go for a cheap feed—the railway station. I thought I could remember where it was. As I strolled down George Street I began to feel beter. It was a mild night and I had a fiver in my pocket, which was a fair sum of money in those days. I lifted my hat, a nondescript felt job, to a couple of young Women in the street and they didn't spit in my eye. There seemed to be a good number of females about, in pairs mostly and probably looking for Yanks, but it wasn't beyond the bounds of possibility that I could acquire some company for the night.

I had a pie and chips at the railway cafeteria and then needed a drink. I went walking in the obvious direction and made the terrible discovery that all the pubs were closed. I'd forgotten—six o'clock closing, the scourge of the Australian drinking man. No doubt there were places where you could get a drink, clubs and such, and sly grog joints, but I didn't know any of them. My spirits were falling with every step. It was beginning to look like a quiet night back in the Metropole with my bottle of Johnnie Walker.

I found myself standing outside a narrow, blank-faced building with heavy glass doors behind which there appeared to be a certain level of gaiety. I could hear music and voices raised in laughter—all in all, exactly my kind of place. I glanced up and saw the plaque in the wall—Journalists' Club. Just then, two taxis pulled up and about ten people, mostly men but with a few women, swarmed out and advanced on the glass doors like a football scrum. They milled around me, laughing and shouting and I struggled to get clear.

'Excuse me,' I said as I trod on some female toes, 'I'm sorry. Can I . . .'

'A Yank,' one of the women screeched. 'It's a civilian Yank. Let's take him in. I've never met a Yank not in uniform before.'

At this there was an enormous hoot of laughter. One of the men planted a kiss on the woman's cheek. 'That line needs work, Doris. You mean you never met a Yank in uniform who *stayed* in uniform longer than four hours.'

Doris giggled and took hold of my arm. 'Six hours, Gordon. I swear it once took me six hours. Don't listen to them, honey. Doris wants you to come in and talk. You can talk, can't you?'

Browning's luck. 'Sure I can talk,' I said.

We surged into the club. Hats and coats were thrown into a closet and a register was signed by one of the men amid much laughter. 'What's your name, buddy?' one of the men asked.

'Richard Browning.'

'And what's your game?'

'I'm an actor.'

'Ooh,' Doris held my arm tighter. 'I caught a live one here.'

We went into the bar and joined the lively crowd of drinkers, singers, darts players and talkers. There must have been a couple of dozen people crammed into the small space and they all seemed intent on getting as much alcohol and nicotine into them as possible. I was introduced around the group, but very little information stuck. Gordon Hardicutt was with the *Herald*, Bruce something was on the *Bulletin*, somebody else was at the *Mirror.* There were a couple who worked for radio stations and one was a cartoonist for *Smith's*,

whatever that was.[19] The women were in the same line of work—
one was a gossip columnist for the *Women's Weekly.*

Gordon bought the first round, which disappeared like a puff of
smoke. The men drank beer, the women port and lemonade or gin
and tonic. It was very pleasant; I could hardly hear a word being
said, but most of the talkers were more interested in what they were
saying than in what was being said to them, so my nods and smiles
were acceptable responses. I offered to buy a round but was firmly
told that only members could buy. It was definitely my kind of
place. After a couple of beers I felt a need to piss and repaired to
the lavatory, which was down a short flight of stairs and smelled
under-sanitised.

I relieved the pressure and washed my hands. A man was standing at the second basin, staring at himself in the mirror. 'When a
lot of remedies are suggested for a disease,' he said, 'that means it
can't be cured.'

'Excuse me?'

'*The Cherry Orchard,*' he said, and I noticed that he had a beautiful mellow voice, even slightly slurred as it was by booze. 'I'd like
to play Chekhov one day.'

That was double-Dutch to me. I dried my hands and got ready
to leave. He grabbed my arm. He was tall and almost cadaverously
thin, but his grip was strong. He had moist brown eyes, like those
of an injured animal. 'Did you say, "Excuse me", meaning "I beg
your pardon"?'

'I guess I did.'

He leaned against the basin, ran water and splashed his face. He
had startlingly high cheekbones, almost like a Cherokee, and his
teeth were very white in a suntanned face.

'I'm an expert on accents,' he said. 'Study 'em, you understand.
Pr'fess'nally. You're not an American.'

'No, I'm an Australian, but I've spent the last twenty years in
the States. You've got a good ear.'

'Good ear, good voice, great talent.'

'Sure,' I said. 'Well, I'll just go up and—'

'What're you doing here, sport?'

'I'm with friends.'

'Name 'em.'

Normally, I'd have told him where to go, but there was something about the eyes and the voice that worked against the drunkenness and belligerence. 'Gordon Hardicutt,' I said.

'Bloody hack.'

I wasn't going to stand for that; Gordon had bought me two drinks. 'And who, may I ask, are you?'

'I'm Peter Finch.'

It means a good deal now—star of *The Pumpkin Eater. Sunday, Bloody Sunday, Network*, posthumous Oscar winner and so on—but it meant nothing then, at least to me.

'Well, I'm Richard Browning and Gordon has been decent to me, so I'll thank you not to run him down. I suggest you sober up and go home.'

'Haven't got a home, 'least, not a real one.'

'You're not alone in that.' I dried my hands on a very dirty towel. 'I'm an actor and know all about it. Good evening.'

'Jus' a minute. Where have you acted? Not here?'

'Well, yes, in a movie or two. But a long time ago. In America more recently. Why?'

'I'm an actor too. Jus' missed a part in a film. Doesn't matter, 'nother one coming up. All Australian films are lousy, anyway.'

I couldn't disagree with that in general, but I said something approving about *Forty Thousand Horsemen.*[20] I'm not in the habit of chatting with strange men in toilets, but there was something about his voice that held me there. It has been commented on many times since. The only movie voice to compare with Finchie's was Burton's—both drunks and whores, of course. Perhaps it's all to do with the testicles.

'All crap,' he said. 'War's nothing like that. War's all about sand and shit and not having enough to drink.'

Hear, hear, I thought, but for someone who looked about nineteen he was too bumptious and full of himself for my liking. 'You know, do you?' I said.

'You bet I know. I've been in the Middle East. Ack-ack gunner. Bloody awful.'

'Wounded?'

'No. On leave. They give me leave to make these bloody awful films.'

He combed his hair, gargled, spat and lit a cigarette. Remarkably, he appeared to sober up in a matter of a few minutes. It was something I saw him do often and it never ceased to amaze me. I saw now that he was older than I'd thought and I began to get the glimmering of an idea.

'Why don't I buy you a drink, Mr Finch, and we can talk about Australian pictures. Ever heard of Harry Southwell?'

'Of course.'

'I worked with him on the Ned Kelly picture.'

He patted his hair into place. He was an actor all right, vain as a peacock. 'Really? Which one?'

'Eh?'

Finch finished his cigarette and wet his lips with his tongue. It was a sign, as I was to learn, that he was ready for a drink. He did it often. 'Southwell made three Kelly films. I hope you weren't in the last one.'

My mind raced. I could hardly admit to being in the 1920 piece of nonsense. That would make me look a real oldster. Apparently the latest effort was nothing to boast about. 'The middle one,' I said.

'That was the best. The other two were crap.²¹ Of course you can buy me a drink.'

We went back up to the bar. Finch appeared to know everyone in the room, especially the women, but he didn't want to join in any of the groups. He was downright rude to Doris as he bustled me into a corner.

She tossed her closely bobbed head. 'Queer,' she said.

Finch ignored her. 'Slip me a quid and I'll get the drinks.'

I wasn't that green, and I knew actors. I gave him ten shillings and he smiled and joked his way through the crush and was back with the drinks in record time.

'Cheers.'

He'd bought double scotches with beer chasers. There was no mention of any change. We drank, he accepted one from my rapidly depleting store of Senior Service and grinned when he saw my Zippo.

'I guess you have spent time in the States,' he said in a very passable American accent.

'And I guess you *are* an actor.'

'You mean you haven't heard of me?'

'I've only been in the country a few days. No, that's not exactly right. A few weeks, call it.'

A characteristic of people like Finchie, people on their way up, is that they are totally uninterested in nonessentials. He didn't need to know anything about my Queensland adventures so he didn't bother to clarify my statement. He drank a slug of scotch and puffed his cigarette. 'I started out as a radio and stage actor,' he said. 'Still pick up a bit of money that way. I've done a few films, but they've all been crap. Nearly all. *The Rats of Tobruk*'ll be out later this year. It's not too bad. But what I really want of course is Britain or Hollywood.'

'Which?' I asked.

He laughed. 'Both. You wouldn't have any proof that you've worked in Hollywood, would you?'

I took out Bobby Silk's letter. The envelope was half-covered by the agency's logo—a golden star with SILK-STEIN picked out in lights on the topmost point. The letterhead was more subdued—a smaller version of the same with the words 'Agency to the Stars' printed underneath in case anyone missed the point. Finch read the letter carefully, threw his head back and laughed uproariously. 'Christ, is it really that bad?'

'Worse,' I said. 'I'd try Britain if I were you.'

We chatted for a while, mostly about the war. I bought more drinks and provided more cigarettes. I wanted to steer him back on to the subject of movie work but the opportunity didn't present. Various people tried to detach Finch but he resisted. I'd seen drinkers like him before. I had the feeling that we'd stay there until my money had run out. I still had two pounds left but I produced a florin and spun it on the wet table top. 'Well's dry, Mr Finch.'

He was drunk again and no wonder. He'd had three doubles and four big glasses of beer. I'd had about half that amount and the room was starting to oscillate. Remember, I was slightly out of practice.

He clinked his glass against mine. 'Peter,' he said.

I saw my chance. 'Richard,' I said. 'Tell me about this film role you missed, Peter.'

'Film about Kingsford-Smith. You know, Smithy. The flyer. Ken Hall's the director. Better than most. Script's OK. That bastard Ron Randell got the part ahead of me. Fuck him.'

'Why'd he get it?'

Finch rearranged his face. Suddenly his chin became squarer and his features more regular. He looked less arresting but more the Hollywood type, something like Gable. He kept the mask in place for a moment and then collapsed into laughter. He held his hands apart like a fisherman demonstrating the size of the one that got away. 'Wider shoulders,' he said.

I laughed. 'And what's this other job you've got lined up?'

He shrugged. 'Piece of crap. Funny thing, Randell's in it too. Give me a chance to show him up.'

A true professional, Finchie. He outlined the plot of the film to me—an unlikely story of a son taking revenge on his faithless mother by marrying and then deserting her stepdaughter by a later marriage, his stepsister.

'Jesus,' I said. 'Sounds bad.'

'You haven't heard the half of it, sport. I'm supposed to play Randell's father, and he's two years older than me.'

'That's a problem. You could pass for twenty.'

Doris overheard this on her way out. She lifted one shoulder and flapped one wrist. 'Pansies,' she said.

CHAPTER FOURTEEN

I must admit that something of the doubt Doris had raised entered my mind when Finch invited me back to his flat. On the other hand, he had no money and I was pretending to have none, so perhaps it was all above board. We staggered out of the club and Finch set off deliberately in an easterly direction.

'Where's your place?'

'Kings Cross. Bit of a walk, but I could get there blind, I mean blindfolded.'

That joke carried us along for a few blocks. It had been a good many years since I'd staggered drunk through the streets of Sydney, but some things hadn't changed. Instinctively, we avoided the dark lanes where danger might lurk and we lifted our hats to women who looked at us with disgust. There were plenty of servicemen about, including a lot of Americans—fresh-faced, wearing well-pressed uniforms and many with a girl on the arm.

'Good chaps, Americans,' Finch said. 'Friendly, good manners. I'd like to work there.'

I thought of some of the people I knew in Hollywood. They were about as friendly as King Kong and their manners were worse. I grunted and concentrated on not being shouldered off the foot-path by a band of half-drunk sailors singing 'Waltzing Matilda'. I realised that Finch was humming along and pretty much in tune. He seemed to be in the process of sobering up again.

'Here we are, old sport,' he said, producing a couple of keys on the end of a piece of string. The string was attached to his braces. We had made several turns away from the bright main street and stood outside a small block of flats in a dark cul-de-sac. He unlocked a door that opened into a small entrance hall.

'Up one.' Finch sprang up the stairs like a ten-year-old. I plodded up after him, feeling my years and reflecting that God only knew what he was like when he was rested and sober.

Finch unlocked another door and entered the flat, snapping on lights and still humming. The flat was small with a sitting room, one bedroom and a tiny kitchen. The first piece of furnishing I saw put my mind at rest—it was a framed photograph of an extraordinarily beautiful woman. She had high cheekbones, slanted eyes and a sensuous mouth.

Finch smiled when he saw me staring. 'My wife,' he said. 'Weren't worried by what that slag Doris said, were you? Not interested in men. Plenty of offers, but just not interested. You?'

'The same. I'm married too. Wife's Chinese. Yours looks a bit . . .'

'Russian. Tamara Tchinarova. Dancer.'

I glanced towards the bedroom door. It was hard to imagine why a man would spend his time boozing at the Journalists' Club with a woman like that to come home to. 'Is she here?'

Finch, who had thrown his hat and jacket on a chair and lit a cigarette from a packet he'd found on a shelf, shook his head. 'Away on tour. Dancing in some god-forsaken country hole. Fancy a drink?'

'Have you got any coffee?'

'"Fraid not. Bloody stuff's unprocurable. Tea?'

'I'll have a drink.'

He found two bottles of beer in the ice chest and ripped the tops off both—that was Finchie. We settled down to drink them, smoke the remaining cigarettes and try to get to what each wanted of the other.

'What's going on in the movie business here just now, Peter?'

Finch waved his glass expansively without spilling a drop. 'As usual, this and that. Always some nut wanting to produce, direct, put up money. The army's reasonable. Local films're good for morale, don't y'know.'

'I've done most things—act, stunts, unit direction, even a bit of scripting. Think there might be some work for me?'

That was stretching it a bit, but I certainly had some idea of what those jobs involved. It wasn't what Finch wanted to hear though. He frowned and stubbed out his cigarette.

'Small beer, old chap. What's keeping you away from . . . what's his name, Silkstein, and Hollywood?'

'You read the letter, Peter. I was on a sort of hush-hush mission that went wrong. I'm in bad odour with the Australian army.'

Finch's fluid laughter rippled out. 'Well, I'm no stranger to that. But I was hoping you'd be a useful contact, stateside.'

'I might be. I've worked with F . . .' I was about to say Fairbanks, but that was ancient history. It stuck in my craw, but I said, 'Flynn, and some of the other big names. I taught Gary Cooper to shoot.'

'Did you teach him to fuck?'

'No, Peter. I think he was pretty good at that already.'

More laughter, more beer, more tobacco. Peter told me about being in Darwin when the Japanese bombers came over and about his experiences in the Middle East. I told him about Queensland and Lieutenant Okano and Harry and all the rest.

'That's a great story,' he said. 'War stuff's all the go just now. Thought of writing it down?'

'Well . . .'

'Tell you what. I'm due to meet Eric Porter[22] tomorrow to talk about this film we're doing. He's the director and producer. How about you come along and we'll . . . what d'they say in Hollywood?'

'Pitch it to him.'

'That's right. We'll pitch it to him.'

He'd found some Russian brandy brought in by one of Tamara's people, and by this time Finch was doing a perfect imitation of my accent, which was a mish-mash of Australian, British and Californian with the American predominating. I'll swear it was the voice he used in *Network*, but that was a long, sad way ahead. We agreed on the strategy and I struggled to my feet with the floor feeling decidedly insecure beneath them.

'Got somewhere to go, old man?'

'Metropole.'

'Oh, good pub. Nice place.'

'Only f'r t'night.'

'You pop along here, Roslyn Flats, in the morning. Drop your kit. We'll have breakfas' in the Cross and see Eric for lunch. Always sting the producer for lunch, right, Dick?'

'Right, Peter.'

How I made it back to the Metropole through the dark, dangerous streets of wartime Sydney, I'll never know. Perhaps homing pigeons are drunk on something carried by the wind. It's as good a theory as any, and the only way I can explain how I came to wake up in the hotel bed, with my head beating like a speedball, somewhere around nine a.m. the next morning. I was even half undressed, wearing my shirt, tie and underpants, and when I dived for my trousers, which were in a heap on the floor, I found that the small amount of money I'd saved from the raging thirst of Peter Finch was intact.

Don't let anybody tell you that the time to do a flit from a hotel is at night. Nonsense. The time is in the morning, when the fresh staff are still imagining that most people are honest and that a big tipper might happen along at any minute. The secret is to make sure that the hotel guests are at breakfast. All defences are down. I was roughly shaved, half washed, and almost sober when I slipped out of a back door of the Metropole Hotel and threw myself into the no-man's land of Sydney, Australia, in October 1944.

When I arrived, Peter was sitting on the tiny balcony of his flat, drinking tea.

'Don't like this stuff, do you?' he said. 'Sorry, there's nothing else, I'm afraid.'

I said it didn't matter although I would have given a lot for a cup of coffee. It's difficult to convey the way things were in those days in Australia. Not many people had refrigerators and none, as far as I could see, ever had chilled juice in them. What they called coffee was made by heating a mixture of coffee and chicory essence, sweet gooey stuff, with equal parts of water and milk. The Finch flat didn't have a toaster, and Peter was eating thick slices of bread with butter and jam. In a properly conducted household there would be a supply of homemade cakes and biscuits, but my guess was that the bread and jam was the only food available chez Finch.

'Got a smoke?' Peter said. 'We went through all mine last night.'

I had two Senior Service left. We lit up. Finch was wearing an army greatcoat as a dressing gown over his underwear, which was none too clean. He hadn't a bean in the world and he couldn't have cared less. I've always admired this attitude but am of a rather more anxious disposition myself.

'So, are we going to see Porter?'

Peter puffed smoke. 'D'you know you can glimpse the water through there?' He pointed at two apartment blocks on the other side of the street. 'This is a beautiful city. You can't see it properly from here, but wait till you get on the water.'

'Are we going on the water?'

'Ferry to Milsons Point. I hope you've got a few bob.'

I nodded.

Peter smiled. 'Thought you might have. Don't worry, I'll hit old Eric up for a quid or two. We'll be right.'

Ten minutes later, with Finch waved, shaved and wearing sports clothes which, in those days, meant simply that your jacket had fewer buttons than a suit coat and the pants didn't match, we were walking in the direction of Circular Quay. Women stared at Peter and he acknowledged every glance with a bright smile. It was as if he was promising to give each and every one of them a quick tumble sooner or later. I was taller and more solidly built, but with my ill-fitting suit and the grey in my hair I wasn't in Peter's league. Give me an hour with a good Rodeo Drive men's outfitter and barber and I flatter myself I'd have given him a run for his money. But it was poor cousin time for Browning just then.

It was a warm spring morning and we both had our coats off and our hats back on our heads by the time we reached the Quay.

'How about a quick one before we go over?' Peter proposed.

The quick one, at a pub opposite the ferry wharf, turned into several slow ones and it was close to midday before we got on the boat. I can't think of a city that looks better from the water than Sydney. The bridge took my attention of course, but the whole scene was magic, with the small boats playing about in the light breeze and the big white houses on the hills saying, 'Look at me. Don't you wish you could afford me?' Finch and I sat on the outside benches, clearing our heads of the beer and smoke fumes.

'Good to be alive, eh, Dick?'

'Right,' I said, pointing to the mansions, 'but better to be alive and rich.'

'One of these days,' he said. 'One of these days.'

All right for him, at twenty whatever he was, but I was a lot further down the track and I had exactly four shillings and sixpence in my pocket. Finch had suddenly gone moody on me. He stood by the rail with his hands deep in his trouser pockets.

'What's the matter?' I asked.

'I should be back with my mates in Darwin, or in the Middle East. Instead, I'm poncing around making these stupid films. It doesn't seem right.'

'You say the government *wants* you to make films.'

He spat into the water, a very un-Finchlike thing to do. 'The government,' he sneered. 'A pack of running dogs, sucking up to the Americans. Just you wait and see, when the war's over they'll get the boot and Menzies and his mob'll be down on the unions and all for letting the capitalists have a free go.'

Finchie posed as a radical in those days, a hater of the system. Perhaps it wasn't a pose, but it never stopped him pursuing his own career ruthlessly and tramping on anyone who got in his way. In any case, it was lucky for me—my story about being more or less on the run from Military Intelligence had a strong appeal for him. As we docked at the Milsons Point wharf, his gloom seemed to lift.

'I like it over here,' he said. 'I think Tamara would too. I think we might move.'

'Why not?' I said. I filed away for future reference the insight that thoughts of his wife cheered him up. Exactly the reverse, you might say, of my situation.

We climbed the steps from the wharf and walked up a steep street away from the water. Peter had already told me that Eric Porter had a solid reputation as a maker of documentaries and shorts and that he had an ambition to move on into feature films. It was a comfort that he knew which way a camera pointed; in Hollywood, not all of the guys with the same ambition did. We stopped outside a block of flats which had nothing to recommend them except the view. Finch whistled piercingly and a man put his head out of a second storey window.

'I wish you wouldn't do that, Peter. Marjorie's asleep. She was up with one of the children all night.'

'Sorry, Eric,' Finch said. 'Come down and we'll go for a walk. I want to talk about *The Sun is Warm.*'

'*A Son is Born,*' the man I took to be Eric Porter said.

'I'm tired,' I said to Finch. 'Can't we go in and sit down?'

'Are you mad? And catch some revolting childhood disease? No fear.' He gestured emphatically for Porter to come down. The head was withdrawn and Finch leaned against the gatepost. He patted his pockets. 'Blast. Out of smokes. Well, Eric'll see us right. Just help me keep him talking. Don't say anything negative. I'll steer him to the pub and we'll be set for lunch and a few pots.'

Porter was a tall, thin man with spectacles and a stoop. Finch introduced me but Porter barely acknowledged my presence. He walked briskly so that I had to struggle to keep up. Finch kept pace easily enough. We stayed on the high ground, skirting a headland with a magnificent harbour view and a very pleasant park. The sun was hot and the shade was inviting. Porter ignored all these things and talked non-stop.

'I think I've got McCallum for Selden,' he said.

Finch nodded. 'Good. He'll be fine. Have you cut any of those "darlings" out of the script yet?'

'A few. But it's a good script. We're all very happy with it.'

'It's OK, but there's too many "darlings".'

'It's a sophisticated piece.'

'Sophisticated people say darling a lot, do they?' Finch propelled Porter towards a set of steps. To my great relief, I could see the pub at the bottom. 'Is that right, Dick? I wouldn't know.'

'Some do,' I said. 'And some don't. Are you trying for a British feel for the film?'

Porter stopped dead in his tracks. 'Good God, no. Just the opposite. I want an American feel, you might say—pacy and with a sense of plenty of money about. For some of the scenes, that is.'

'I might be able to help you there,' I said.

CHAPTER FIFTEEN

The Military Inn at Milsons Point did a very good fried fish lunch. I hadn't had any breakfast and fell on the plate when it arrived. Porter picked at his food; Finch ate heartily, but was more interested in the beer. The day had turned cool suddenly, with the wind swinging around to the south. We sat in the Ladies Lounge, which was where they served food in Australian hotels in those days. Not all of the women in the room were ladies, and I could feel eyes being drawn to Finch. His responses were lazy. He waved to a few people he evidently knew but did not invite them to join us.

'What do you think, Peter?' Porter said sharply.

'There's a way around it.'

Here again, Finch amazed me. I'd been busy getting the last few chips down and I hadn't paid much attention to what Porter had been saying—something about the difficulties of the similarity in age between Finch and Ron Randell. I'd have sworn that Peter was taking less in than me, but he hadn't missed a beat.

'Just don't have 'em appearing in the same scene.'

'But we see them getting into the car together when Paul Graham's drunk and—'

'Cut it,' Finch said. 'Or if you think you need it, shoot it from an angle that doesn't show their faces. Hell, shoot it from ground level. What does it matter?'

'Peter, this film is terribly important to me.'

Finch was studying a redhead in a white dress.

'It's important to me, too, Eric. I need the money.'

Porter sighed and sipped some beer. 'They *have* to be together in the deathbed scene.'

'That doesn't matter. Slap some paleface all over me. Make me look a hundred. I don't care. Anyway, Eric, you have to understand that it's all an illusion. A man is dying, people think of him as older than his son who's sitting there scratching his balls. People's imaginations do the work. Isn't that right, Dick?'

'Right,' I said.

Like everybody, Porter had a breaking point. He'd been sitting there feeding these two, watching them sop up drink he was paying for, and now they were high-hatting him. 'What exactly do you know about anything, Mr Browning?'

Finch grinned and rubbed the side of his nose. 'He's a secret service agent, Eric. Very hush-hush. Before that, he worked in Hollywood.'

'Hollywood.'

'Show him the letter, Dick.'

I fished out Bobby Silk's letter and handed it to Porter while Peter scooped up some of the change and went to the bar. Porter's hostility faded as he read.

'Remarkable,' he said. 'Are you going back to ah . . . take up this offer?'

I swilled the last inch of my beer. 'In time.'

'What's your connection with Peter?'

'Oh, we just sort of met and got along well. He's interested in Hollywood and—'

'I *need* him for my next feature. It's all planned.'

'Got a contract?'

'No, but . . .'

'Eric,' I said. 'I think we can do business.'

By the time Finch got back, Porter and I had made a deal. I was to go on the payroll at eight pounds a week with the job of scouting locations, advising on costumes and set decoration and anything else that might come along. I was also to use my best efforts to keep Finch in Australia for the filming of *Storm Hill*, Porter's next film and certain masterpiece. Porter advanced Finch twenty pounds and me four against our wages. Then he had to get back to his wife and sick child.

'Fancy a walk back across the bridge?' Finch said.

Well rested, and with a full load of food and beer on board, it seemed like a good idea to me. We set off, wearing our jackets now against the cold wind and having to keep our heads properly angled to keep our hats on. This is a skill that has been lost. You never see a man now who knows how to keep his hat on in a wind.

'Well, how did you make out, Dick?' Finch said as we neared the approach to the footway over the bridge.

'You saw. Four quid and a job, of sorts.'

Finch laughed. 'No, I mean what sort of a deal did you do with him about me? Did you undertake to keep me sober, to stick to the script, what?'

Finch was a shrewdie and he never expected anyone to have better ethics than his own. There was no point in lying to him, he'd have seen straight through me. 'I said I'd try to keep you here for his next movie. To go quiet on the "I can help you in Hollywood" stuff.'

'That's a pretty good arrangement. I'm not planning to pop off to America just yet. Good on you.'

'You don't object?'

A gust of wind buffeted us as we moved up onto the footway. We gripped out hats. 'Old son,' Finch said, 'I may be an irresponsible, pinko pisspot, but I'm a realist. The strong in this world do what they have to do. They have only one duty in my book.'

'And what's that, Peter?'

'To look after the weak.'

We tramped across the narrow walkway, high above the water, which was churning and frothing as the wind whipped it up. There were fewer boats on the harbour now, and they seemed to be heading for cover. There was a steady flow of cars going both ways and a few trains roared past. I glanced up anxiously at the sky; neither of us was dressed for rain and the clouds were getting darker.

'Don't do that!' Finch said sharply.

'What?'

'Look up like that. It reminds me of Darwin and those bloody Jap planes coming in.'

'Bad, was it?'

'I was shit-scared. Much worse than a first night, I can tell you. And that's bad enough.'

He was an actor, you see, living on his nerves and wits, never knowing whether the next moment was going to bring triumph or disaster. It takes a terrible toll and Finch, even then, was showing some of the signs. We crossed the bridge and he needed a pub, despite my belief that it was going to rain.

'Wet inside's the best antidote to wet outside,' he said. He was given to remarks like that, and I suppose they helped him to handle the Oscar Wilde role. I once heard him say, 'The best cure for one woman is another woman, or two,' but that was much later, in Ceylon in fact.[23]

We had a few drinks in a pub in Kent Street where, remarkably, Finch seemed not to know anyone. 'Dull place this,' he said.

'D'you mean the pub, or Australia?'

'Oh, Australia's all right, at least for the time being, but I would like to get to Britain.'

My mind was running on my own experiences: I remembered working on Longford's *Bounty* movie, a good many years but not so many miles away.[24] Thoughts of Bligh and the mutiny naturally lead in one direction. 'Well,' I said idly, 'that's where Flynn went at first. Before he became a star in Hollywood.'

Finch sat bolt upright. His deeply sunken eyes seemed to burn in their sockets. 'Flynn, did you say? Are you comparing me with Errol Flynn?'

'Well, no, Peter, it's just that he knocked around a bit, like you, and—'

'The man's a mountebank,' Finch said. 'He can't act for shit. All he can do is flash his teeth and swing from ropes, like a monkey.'

'No argument from me,' I said hastily. 'But he's certainly made it big in the movies. What actors do you admire, Peter?'

Finch drained his drink. 'Olivier,' he said.

For next few weeks I did nothing much except lounge around Finch's flat where I was sleeping on the couch, drink beer, go for long walks through Sydney and, as the weather warmed up, swim at the Redleaf sea baths. I became tanned and fit and, instead of darkening my hair, I helped along what the sun had already started by bleaching it. I kept the moustache, but by late October I didn't look much like the Dick Kelly who'd emerged from the Queensland bush. After one or two visits, I stayed away from the Journalists' Club—there were too many inquisitive types there, men and women hungry for a story. In a way, Sydney was starved of news. The war provided the headlines week in and week out, and readers were keen for human interest stories. I didn't want to be one of them.

Of course, I kept my eyes open for any expressions of interest in me, watched my back, kept well clear of the Metropole Hotel, avoided getting drunk in public and so on. 'Oily Feathers' had struck me as a pretty shrewd operator, and I knew from my own brief career as a detective how easy it is to find someone if you really try.[25] Finch had a wide circle of friends and, although I was occasionally in the company of actors like Hal Lashwood and John McCallum, I tried to avoid them as much as possible. Actors drink and talk too much, and it was likely that Featherstonhaugh would have an ear to the thespian ground.

I was more comfortable with Peter's army buddies, who arrived at the flat with Gladstone bags full of beer and left when all the bottles were empty. A few were long-term AWOL cases. Finch was not sanctimonious about these men, saying that he might very well have done a bunk himself if he hadn't had the luck to get long 'other essential duties' leave. I never told him about my 1918 desertion, but the feeling that he would have understood helped me to like him all the more. The military police called at the flat once and Peter had his papers ready for inspection in a flash. He might sometimes have looked like a disorganised drunk, but he handled the essentials neatly. I had a bad scare on that occasion, thinking that the MPs might have come for me, but they were looking for 'one of our blokes' and scarcely gave my Canadian documents a glance.

I ran short of money and Finch came up with the solution. 'Give Eric a ring,' he said, 'and tell him you think I'm getting itchy feet. He'll come across.'

I did it, suggesting that I could talk Finch round, and mentioning that I'd found a great location for some outdoor scenes. Porter sent me a cheque.

'An actor's business is to get money out of producers,' Finch said, as we knocked a few spots off the cheque in a Darlinghurst pub.

'And what's a producer's business, Peter?'

'God knows. To get bums on seats perhaps. Not many are much good at it.'

Early in November I travelled to Newcastle on the train and walked down to the beach. Much had changed, but this was where I'd sewed some wild oats and acquired some scars, and memory guided my feet accurately. I hadn't seen the family house since I'd made an attempt to get past the guard dogs before I stowed away aboard the *Sternwood* in 1920, but I knew exactly where to find it—on the hill overlooking the beach. 'Wild Bill' had chosen the site and the pretentious, sprawling design of the house to show the old-money Novocastrains that he was every bit as good as they were, as well as tougher and richer.

The day was warm and there was a stiff breeze coming off the water. My head was full of memories, sweet and sour, as I followed the concrete path around the beachfront. The old sea baths were showing signs of wear and tear; the facade needed a coat of paint and the admission prices had almost worn away. I looked closely, trying to read the figures. It looked like twopence for adults and a penny for children, but that couldn't be true any more. I turned around to look at the house and experienced a shock like a punch in the solar plexus. The house wasn't there. The driveway, the garden, the stables and the ugly red brick pile itself were all gone. The hill was occupied by a hospital.

I leaned back against the sea baths' wall and lit a cigarette with a shaking hand. Somehow, you expect the house you grew up in to endure forever, even if, as in my case, you half hated it and fled from it as soon as you could. You may change but it shouldn't, at least not too much. To see it swept away altogether shook me. I was suddenly aware that people were looking at me. I had been oblivious of them, but things were coming back into focus. I straightened up and took a few brave puffs on my fag. *So what if it's gone?* I thought. I remembered 'Wild Bill's' drunken rages and his whistling strap. My mother's gentle, useless pleas. *If you think I'm going to make a pilgrimage to the cemetery you've got another think coming.*

I caught the first train back to Sydney.

When I got to the flat I found Finch tidying up. This was something I hadn't seen him do before and I watched in amazement as he attempted to dust the top of a bookcase. 'Tamara's coming back,' he said. 'Due in tonight. You'll have to move out I'm afraid.'

There was no arguing with that. The flat was definitely a three's-a-crowd kind of place. I gave Peter a hand with the dishes, which meant washing every single cup, saucer, plate and glass in the place. We had rather let the housekeeping go. When we'd finished, only breaking two or three pieces as I recall, Peter shook my hand and practically pushed me out the door.

'Got to clean myself up, too. Best of luck, Dick. Be seeing you.'

I shouldered my kitbag, bought a paper and made for the nearest pub. Turning to the 'rooms to let' section I got my third shock for the day—rents in Sydney had skyrocketed. A furnished room in a good suburb cost as much as three pounds a week and the ones at the rate I was interested in, around the one pound mark, did not sound promising: 'attic room', 'sleep-out', 'veranda room' and so on. I was tired after my long and distressing day, but I began the tramp from house to house. I'd marked myself out an acceptable area— Kings Cross, Woolloomooloo, Darlinghurst, Paddington—but my spirits began to fall after the first few enquiries. The rooms I liked, with a bit of space and light and reasonable facilities, I couldn't afford and the ones I could afford were flea traps.

I inspected floors so covered in cockroaches that they seemed to move, walls that dripped moisture, boarded-up porches, landings lit by low watt light globes and cellars that required wellington boots to negotiate.

'Not la-di-da enough for you, eh, Yank?' was the standard reaction when I suggested that these places weren't fit for pigs. Slatternly landladies and men with beer bellies that made it hard to get by them on the stairs mocked me and made it clear that if I didn't take the room someone else would. After a couple of hours of this I ended up outside a narrow terrace in Crown Street, Darlinghurst. I was hungry, my feet were sore and I was feeling ill from some of the foul air I'd breathed. I knocked and lowered my bag wearily to the pavement.

'Yeah?' The voice came from above. I looked up. The balcony overhung the footpath.

'I've come about the room.'

'You a Yank?'

I'd suspected that being taken for an American had inflated the prices of the rooms I'd been shown. After rejecting yet another rat hole I lost my temper. 'No, for Christ's sake,' I shouted. 'I'm a bloody Australian!'

'All right, all right, don't do your block. Hang on and I'll let you in.'

I caught the glimpse of a female face and the flick of red, silky fabric. That's how I came to meet Ushi and to live in a brothel.

CHAPTER SIXTEEN

Ursula Tanvier was half French and half German.

'The top half is French and the bottom half is German,' she used to say. She had a small face framed by dark hair. Her brown eyes were huge. She had small, high, hard breasts, slender arms and a small waist. Then she expanded; her hips were wide and her bottom generous. Her legs, although shapely, were large. I found these odd proportions very erotic—physical perfection has never counted greatly with me, although it's agreeable when it happens along. When women's characteristics are at issue, give me a loving disposition every time. That's what Ushi had, in buckets.

She showed me the room—a pleasant, spacious, scrupulously clean one at the back of the house with a view towards Hyde Park. Ushi was wearing a red satin dressing gown with a long skirt. Her hair was still wet from washing and she had no makeup on. She was quite tall in her bare feet, and I was somewhat discomforted by the way she looked at me—like a casting director surveying a bunch of extras.

Eventually she smiled, leaned back against the wall on the landing outside the room and said, 'One pound per week.'

'It's great. I'll take it. I can't understand why it's still available. The ad's been in the paper all day.'

'Lots of triers,' she said. 'You're only the second bloke I've let in. I told the others the room had already gone.'

I put my kitbag on the double bed, a solid-looking brass job, and turned to face her. 'How come?'

'Me 'n Pam're working girls. Pam lives here with me. D'you know what I mean?'

Tricky, I thought. *Don't want to jump to the wrong conclusion, but don't want to look dumb either.* I recalled the sitting room I'd glimpsed on the way to the stairs—a red velvet sofa and a big, gilt-framed mirror. The scent in the air wasn't from roses and, although Ushi was without makeup, her finger and toenails were painted the brightest red I'd ever seen.

I shrugged and opted for honesty. 'I think I know what you mean. You entertain men here. I'm broadminded. This is the best room for the price I've seen and I want it. I'll be out a lot. I won't get in your way.'

'That's not it. We want a man around, but we don't want him bludging off us.'

'I've got a job.'

'Good. You're big. How old are you?'

'Forty.'

'You look it. Been in the war?'

I nodded. Well, I had been, in a way. 'I was in the Canadian army. But I'm an Australian, like I told you. How about you?'

Something about her face and movements made me ask. That was when she told me she was half French and half German, but not the rest of it. 'Suppose Pam or me struck a bit of bother, would you help out?'

I had a good deal of experience of brothels in my younger days, and I knew that most clients were nervous or drunk or both. A man with his pants on has a big advantage over one with them off. I removed my hat and gave her a half bow. 'I'd be happy to.'

'OK. I'm Ushi Tanvier. Who're you?'

'Dick Browning.'

She put her hand out and I shook it. She smiled at me, showing slightly protuberant, slightly gapped teeth. I was starting to find everything about her arousing. She pulled her hand free and turned it palm up. 'A quid in advance,' she said.

I paid her, which left me very little money in hand. She gave me a latchkey and showed me the bathroom and kitchen. The whole house was spotless and, if it was slightly overdone in the mirrors and soft furnishings department, I wasn't going to object.

'D'you cook, Dick?' Ushi asked.

'No.'

'Good. Me'n Pam usually have our evening meals out in the line of business, and we don't eat much other times on account of our figures. Also, we don't want to stink the place up with snags and onions and such.'

'The smelliest thing I make is coffee,' I said. 'Not that there's any coffee around just now.'

'Oh, we can get plenty from the Yanks. Look, we've got some now.'

She opened a cupboard and showed me several large, unopened packets of PX coffee. She told me that one of Pam's customers had given her a percolator, which she'd never got around to using. I opened the box, assembled it and had coffee perking on the gas stove in no time flat. We sat in the kitchen, drank our coffee and talked about America. Ushi had heard a lot about it and wanted to go there. She asked me questions like, 'What does a hamburger taste like?' and I tried to tell her. It was fun. Then the telephone rang. She spoke briefly, gulped the rest of her coffee and went into a mad rush from her bedroom to the bathroom and back again about ten times. When she left she was wearing a green silk dress and a white wrap, seamed stockings, gold shoes with high heels and I was jealous and in love.

I went out for a meal, spent some money on beer and cigarettes, and returned to the empty Crown Street house. I've always been an incurable snoop and I took a good look through Ushi's room. I would have investigated Pam's too, except that it was locked. Ushi possessed a lot of clothes, shoes and make-up and very little else. Her private papers consisted of the usual things—baptismal certificate, some school reports and photographs, a diary with only a couple of entries, some documents relating to her mother's hospitalisation and death from influenza in 1919. Ushi, I calculated, could only have been a child at the time. A newspaper clipping, undated, recounted her success in an interschool swimming carnival—Ursula Tanvier had won the under-fifteen 50 metres and 100 metres races in freestyle and breaststroke and had finished second in the diving competition. It seemed to be the only record of her teenage years she cared to keep.

I drank my beer and went to bed early, tired after the accommodation-seeking tramp. Ushi and Pam could have returned home with Americans or Hindustanis for all I knew. After several weeks on Finch's lumpy couch, I slept deeply, peacefully and very late in the big, soft brass bed.

The first person I encountered in the morning, what little was left of it, was Pam. She was a redhead, as a matter of choice rather than nature, with a bright friendly smile below eyes as hard as prison bars.

'Hi, big boy,' she said. 'Ushi reckons you make great coffee.'

'That's right. You must be Pam.'

'Pamela Walker. No jokes about streets, if you please. Make us a pot now, would you, love? I had a hell of a night. He had me out dancing—which is to say, trying to keep my feet from being squashed—and drinking bloody champagne, till two a.m.'

I made the coffee and she drank a cup so hot it would have scalded my throat. She didn't seem to notice.

'Oh, that's good. You're a treasure. Got a cigarette?'

I gave her one and we both lit up. She was small and neatly built and sat very straight, although she looked tired. Her hair was hanging down to her shoulders and her face was very pale. I put her in the mid-thirties with the clock ticking fast. She wore Chinese-style pyjamas with a high collar and mules.

'Where's Ushi?' I asked.

'What's today? Friday? She's out at Waverley visiting her mother's grave. Always does that of a Friday morning, rain, hail or shine. She'll be back soon. Well, ta for the coffee. I have to go and see my Friday afternoon fella.'

Soon after Ushi came in, wet from a sudden spring shower. I told her I'd met and liked Pam. Then I made coffee and we sat in the kitchen and talked, which she was in a mood to do. She told me about her French mother coming out to South Australia to work as a governess for a wealthy German family.

'Old story,' she said. 'Herr whatever his name was got her pregnant and kicked her out. She came to Sydney, had me and died in the 'flu epidemic after the war.'

I had witnessed the ravages of that epidemic in Europe and could sympathise. I didn't tell Ushi that though—I was only supposed to be forty years of age, remember. Instead, I asked what had happened to her. 'You must have been very young.'

She nodded. 'I was three. I was fostered out. I don't remember her and I don't even have a picture of her. Some relations from France wrote to me years after and what they told me is all I know.'

'She must have been an educated woman. The family should have looked after you.'

'The chap who wrote said they lost everything in the war. They didn't want to have anything to do with me. I think Mum must have been a bit of a black sheep.'

She told me that the foster homes had been bad.

'When I was little it was all right. They clucked over me. Then I grew up this funny shape.'

'Your shape looks fine to me.'

She was too deep in memories to notice my tone or to take offence. 'I hated school. Nuns, Christ, how I hate nuns! I was a lot of trouble, so I was sent back to the orphanage. Got taken on twice more. The first pair wanted a slave, the second time the man wanted somewhere to wet his wick. I shot through, worked at this and that and ended up here. Jesus, I haven't talked like that in years. Must be the coffee on top of visiting Mum. Always makes me soppy.'

I offered her a cigarette, which she refused.

'I like the smell, but I can't stand inhaling the smoke. Go ahead though, Dick. I must say you're a good listener. What's your story?'

I gave her an edited version, heavy on the Hollywood stuff, very light on the rest. I smoked only one cigarette. We moved on from coffee to brandy and coffee, and then to brandy neat. She told me that her American of the night before had left her at the door with a handshake.

'He decided he loved his wife too much to spend the night with me. Can you imagine that?'

'No,' I said. 'I can't.'

'You married, Dick?'

I told her a little about May Lin, but not about the others. I was genuinely confused about my current marital status.[26]

'I don't know,' I said. 'The way it is in Los Angeles, it's hard to tell.'

'I'd love to go there.'

'I'd love to take you.'

'Would you, Dick? Would you really?'

By this time, she'd shucked off her raincoat and her hair had dried into a ring of curls around her face. She was wearing a red blouse and a black skirt. Her eyes glittered from the brandy, and something else. I leaned across and kissed her wide, soft mouth. She kissed me back and, although I was half drunk, I knew enough about kissing to tell that this wasn't professional. Our tongues thrust and writhed together like snakes.

'Ushi,' I gasped, 'I want you.'

'Well, take me, big boy. Take me.'

I stood and she did the same. We gripped each other—bum, breasts and crotch—then rushed out of the kitchen, up the stairs, towards the back of the house. She led the way and the sight of her big hips and buttocks rolling in front of me made me pant with lust. I caught her on the landing and swept her towards my room and the big brass bed.

Her fingers clawed at the buttons of her blouse as I was stripping off my shirt. 'Pam?' she said.

I spun her around and unhooked her brassiere. 'With her fella.'

Ushi pushed my hands away, freed her breasts and lay back on the bed, unbuttoning her skirt.

'Good on her,' she said. 'Good on her. Come on, Dick. Come on!'

I plunged forward and then it was all nipples and fingers and tongues and hard things and soft things and warm, sweet rushes of love.

CHAPTER SEVENTEEN

I wasn't the first man to be romantically involved with a working prostitute and I won't be the last. It isn't as hard a role to play as you might think. The woman swears she gets no pleasure from her trade and the man believes her. Of course she *might* derive the occasional bit of enjoyment, and of course the man *is* jealous, but there are worse problems—such as snoring or frigidity—and Ushi and I got along extremely well, all things considered. For one thing, she met Finch and wasn't attracted to him. This made her a very rare specimen indeed.

'He loves himself too much to love anyone else,' she observed, when I asked her the reason for her apparent indifference to Peter.

'I'm not sure that's true,' I said. 'He's been a good friend to me.'

'Friend, fine. I'm talking about love.'

I left it there. Love was a difficult subject under the circumstances. Only on two occasions did I have to intervene in dealings between Ushi and Pam and their clients. A US Marines colonel got excited one night and wanted to bring his sidearm into the sex play. He was badly out of condition, and I didn't have any trouble getting the Colt .45 automatic, which I kept, away from him. An Australian officer objected to Pam's insistence on him using a condom. He found it amusing to inflate a few and burst them like balloons. Then he got rough and I had to tap him on the skull with a shifting spanner.

He lay sprawled across the bed, naked except for his singlet and socks. Pam began to work on him with her hand.

'What're you doing?' I said.

'When he wakes up he'll have a frenchie on and I'll get my money. Thanks, Dick. You can go now.'

It could have taken the fun and flavour out of sex but it didn't. Ushi and I went at it enthusiastically whenever we could. As I say, I found her unusual proportions unusually exciting—it was like having two different women at the one time, without the complications, if you see what I mean. She was cheerful, as generous with her money as with her body, and we had a hell of a good time through the last months of 1944. It was a cheerful time generally. The war news was all good, with victory in Europe and the Japanese on the run throughout the Pacific.

I did some location scouting for Eric Porter and found a house in Wahroonga that was ideal for the Selden mansion in *A Son is Born*. It had a circular staircase inside and big, opulent rooms. There was a swimming pool and a balcony at the front overlooking a sweeping driveway. The owner was happy to let the place for a few weeks and Porter assigned me the job of finding some suitable cars. The script called for a sports car and a saloon that had to be driven off a cliff and totally wrecked.

'I suppose you'll get an old, rusty one,' Porter said, 'so we can be sure it'll break up. Give it a coat of paint.'

I shook my head. I knew a bit about this sort of thing from my Hollywood days. 'You weaken it by cutting partly through the chassis. I've seen it done. Do you want a fire?'

'Fire? No, David has to survive the crash.'

'OK. No fire. I'll get a car and find someone with an acetylene torch.'

Porter was impressed. He paid me my wages that week, unlike some other weeks. I still saw Finch. He was constantly being offered work on radio, which he accepted when he needed the money, and in the theatre. His army leave seemed to be infinitely extendable and he suffered some guilt over it.

'I should be with the blokes,' he said drunkenly one night in the back room of a Darlinghurst pub where the licensee had an arrangement with the relevant officers of the law.

'You've done your bit, Peter,' I said. 'Another round? Your shout.'

'Too right,' Finch said. He stood to go to the bar and collapsed in a heap. He was very drunk. I helped him up and he went through that transformation I'd seen before. Almost as a matter of will, he appeared to sober up.

'Tamara doesn't understand this,' he said.

'What?'

'Why I go out drinking with my mates. And I can't tell her why.'

I wasn't sure that I understood it myself. Tamara was one of the most beautiful women I'd ever seen—dark-eyed, perfect facial bones, masses of hair. She was slender and her movements were magically graceful, even when she was just pouring a cup of tea.

'Why do you?' I said.

He threw back his head and laughed. 'To stop myself from racing off other women.'

'Tricky,' I said, and I meant it. Finch had what every man dreams of having—an enormous power to attract women—and it brought him more problems than pleasure. Life is strange.

I kept alert, but heard and saw nothing of Oliver Featherstonhaugh and his nasty friends. I made tentative enquiries about the family I had so unwisely married into—the MacKnights of Melbourne. I learned that Elizabeth, my wife, was still alive and running her private hospital in East Melbourne. I drew back from endeavouring to find out if we were still married. Where the MacKnights were concerned, it was better to let sleeping dogs lie. I was on the way to becoming a solid citizen. I applied for, and got, a copy of my birth certificate. I got a driver's licence and opened a bank account. Ushi, as my landlady, signed the papers necessary for me to get a ration book. Almost everything was rationed: bread, meat and milk, tobacco, beer and petrol. Naturally, there was a thriving black market in some of these commodities.

But things were getting easier. Cuffs came back on trousers and shirts had long tails again. Skirts got longer, which was a pity, but bathing suits shrank a bit. Ushi was a keen swimmer and we often went to the baths or to Bondi Beach. I couldn't keep up with her for more than a dozen or so strokes, and it was nothing for her to swim out beyond the breakers and ride some big, booming wave almost back to the beach. She was the only woman I ever saw do such a thing, and she drew some disapproving looks. Ushi didn't care. She rubbed coconut oil on her skin and it rapidly turned brown. We were both keen suntanners.

One day at Bondi she was unusually quiet. She fiddled with her sunglasses, swore when the coconut oil spilled on the newspaper she'd been reading.

'What's the matter?' I said.

'The war's going to end soon, isn't it?'

'Looks that way. Hard to say when.'

'What will you do?'

Careful, Dick. I sifted some sand through my fingers. 'I don't know.'

'Neither do I. The Yanks'll stop coming and then where will I be? Dick, do you think you could get me a part in the film? Maybe I could work in the films.'

I breathed a sigh of relief. 'I can try,' I said.

We started shooting in January in the middle of a heat-wave. It made things difficult—the actors sweated and their makeup ran. They had to wear heavier clothes than were comfortable and tempers frayed. The only scenes they wanted to shoot were the outdoor ones—when Kay Selden and Paul Graham swim and play golf—and Finchie wasn't in any of them. In fact Finch's part, although it offered the best opportunities to show off his acting skills, confined him to the indoors—the small rooms of the Graham flat and the rather unconvincing set they used to suggest a low-life bar. He missed out on the elegance of Wahroonga house scenes and it rankled with him. Still, it helped to give a good, irritable edge to his performance.

Finch played Paul Graham, who marries Laurette in the opening scenes, treats her like dirt, drinks and runs around with other women, causing her to leave him. But they have a son, David, who dotes on his ne'er do well dad, who teaches him to do what he likes—get drunk with the boys and despise his mother. Laurette, played by Muriel Steinbeck, leaves when the snotnosed kid is about fourteen. She divorces Paul Graham and marries her wealthy employer, John Selden, played with great panache by John McCallum. After Paul is killed in a car accident, David, now twenty-one or so, comes to live with the Seldens. The war is on. He hates his mother and stepfather and, to spite them, marries and deserts Selden's daughter, Kay.

For 1945, all this philandering, drinking, divorcing and marrying of a stepsister was pretty racy stuff. With Finch and Randell glowering away, and Muriel projecting buckets of decency while trying not to look too satisfied at landing so nicely on her feet, I had the feeling that the picture was going along well. I was on the payroll as what would have been called a production assistant in Hollywood and worth a screen credit. There was no question of that, however, with Porter.

'You're doing a great job, Dick,' he told me a couple of weeks into the shoot. 'I couldn't do without you, but, you know the problem.'

'Sure, Eric,' I said. 'The unions. Don't worry about it, and you've already made it square with me.'

I meant his agreement to hire Ushi as an extra. She was in the church as a respectable person when Paul and Laurette got hitched, in the bar as a floozie, on the golf links when David and Kay are plighting their troth, and in some crowd scenes. She was thrilled by the whole thing and the rushes showed that the camera liked her. She got along very well with the other cast members and the crew and I was confident that Porter would find something for her in *Storm Hill.*

I told her so in bed one night.

'D'you really think so, Dick? A speaking part?'

'Who knows? Maybe.'

'I *like* working in films. It's fun, even if the money's not much.'

'Everyone likes it, babe,' I said. 'You should see them in Hollywood. They'd kill to get the sort of parts you're looking at. People *have* killed for them.'

'Really, Dick? Tell me.'

I spun her a story about Mabel Normand and Desmond Taylor that *might* have been true.[27] She lapped it up, but Ushi was no fool and the question she put to me next revealed her shrewdness.

'Why don't you want to be in the picture yourself, Dick? Eric'd give you a part, wouldn't he? With these war scenes coming up, you'd be perfect.'

True enough, but I didn't want my face, however disguised, appearing in giant size on screens around Australia. For all I knew, 'Oily Feathers' and Elizabeth MacKnight Browning were keen picture-goers. I made some joking remark about being shy and we got back to doing what we'd been doing before—more fun than talking, as I recall.

The shoot progressed smoothly. My only problem was getting hold of a suitable car to arrange the crash scene. It had to be a decent-looking vehicle and it was to finish as a total wreck. Porter didn't want me to spend too much money on it and I was spending a good bit of time scouting the used-car dealers. The scene could be shot at any time, but Porter became anxious to get it in the can. He was moving into one of the more interesting parts of the picture, where footage he shot in bushland outside Sydney was to be blended with stuff shot in New Guinea by the famous war cinematographer Damien Parer. The Parer material was gritty—battered-looking diggers scanning the skies, waiting for the mail, carrying wounded comrades through the jungle. The New Guinea village set looked realistic enough as far as I could tell, and everyone was interested in the work. Ushi was playing one of the nurses dealing with the wounded heroes.

Convinced that he was about to be killed on a dangerous patrol, David Graham wrote Kay a letter apologising for his caddishness and telling her that he loved her. The letter was found clutched in his hand after he was wounded and was conveyed to Kay who, somewhat miraculously, was on the spot. I was busy setting up a Japanese machine-gun nest when Porter sent a messenger to collect me.

'Cecil's not well,' he said.

Cecil Perry was playing a character named Tazzy, a big soldier with winning ways, a mate of David Graham's.

'That's tough,' I said. 'Will you have to reschedule?'

'No, I need him in the next scene but I can keep him in medium shot and he doesn't have a line.'

I was puzzled. Porter got up out of his canvas chair and walked around me, inspecting me like a prize bull.

He made me nervous. 'What the hell are you doing, Eric?'

'You're a dead ringer for Cecil. Darken your hair, put on a moustache and you're perfect.'

'No.'

'Why not? C'mon, Dick, be a pal. Ten quid.'

Finch was standing within earshot, dressed in sports clothes, watching sardonically while the rest of the cast ran around in army singlets with mud on their faces. I couldn't think of a convincing reason to refuse. Hoping to put Porter off, I said, 'Twenty quid.'

'You bastard. Right. Go to make-up.'

I got togged up in a singlet, shorts and boots, let them comb some black muck into my hair and stick on a small moustache, and did the scene. It needed a couple of takes because I was trying to keep my face turned away from the camera as much as possible. Eventually, Porter got what he wanted. I was walking back to the make-up tent when Ushi came running towards me.

'Dick,' she said. 'Oh, Dick, you look so handsome like that. I want to race you off into the bushes.'

'Well . . .'

She pulled free. 'I've got a scene. Don't take it off. Please, Dick, stay like that. I'll make you glad you did.'

Promises in her eyes and her voice. What could I do? I took a look at myself in the mirror and I could see what she meant. Dark suited me better than fair and the moustache *was* handsome. I looked younger, almost the dashing Dick Browning of earlier days. I cleaned myself up a bit and went off again to look for a car to roll down a cliff.

Henderson's car yard was in Ultimo, near the fish markets. It sounded like a good place to pick up a cheap car. In fact I'd been told about the establishment in a pub. My informant had more than hinted that some of Henderson's cars were not necessarily honestly come by. That didn't matter to me, because the vehicle in question was going to be in several widely scattered pieces very soon. The tip was of extra value because where you have a car thief you have an oxywelder, as sure as God made wire coat-hangers to open car doors.

I was driving an old Riley that belonged to Eric Porter's brother, Dudley, who was assistant director on the film. I'd borrowed it to make the trip to Ultimo and Dud was glad to lend it to me for this purpose—he'd feared that his Riley was going to end up as the death car. There wasn't much fat in the budget of *A Son is Born.*

An afternoon shower fell as I went over the Pyrmont Bridge and wound through the wet, narrow streets until I found Henderson's. It was nothing like your modern car lot, with bunting, knee-high fences, life-sized cut-outs of girls in miniskirts and prices written on windscreens. In those days a used car yard was an adjunct to a petrol station or a mechanic's workshop. The typical colour scheme was an oily grey-green and the decor was toolshed functional.

Henderson's was just that sort of place. It stood between two factories. The high cyclone fence in front of the narrow block was topped with a couple of strands of barbed wire and the office inside was a fibro shack with grimy windows and a rusty iron roof. The workshop was like a barn except that there were machines inside instead of animals, and the smell was of oil and petrol instead of hay and cow shit. A dripping sign reading 'Henderson's Mechanical Repairs—All Models' hung above the entrance to the workshop. The wide gate stood open and I drove the Riley through and parked it beside the six cars that stood in a tight formation under a FOR SALE sign tacked up to a post.

I ran my eye over them. A two-tone black and yellow Standard looked a possibility. I lit a cigarette and strolled towards the office, trying to keep clear of the oily puddles that lay in my path. I was aware of being watched from the office. Someone was polishing a peephole in a window. Nothing strange about that. If I ran a hot car yard I'd watch strangers pretty carefully too. I took off my hat and mounted the rickety steps. The door was open and I stepped through it.

'Mr Henderson?'

I couldn't see the man standing back from the window. The light in the room was dim and the visibility was further reduced by a smoke fug. The figure stepped forward to a desk in the middle of the room, but he was still in the shadows. He opened a drawer.

'I'm Henderson.'

'My name's Browning. I've been told—'

'Your name's William Hughes,' he said. 'And I'm going to blow your fuckin' head off.'

He stepped around the desk and into the light. I was looking into the eyes of Jack Henderson, my former comrade in arms whom I'd deserted in France in 1918 and later bashed over the head with a truncheon on the Sydney to Newcastle train.[28]

CHAPTER EIGHTEEN

It was Jack's son of course. I realised this within seconds, but the likeness was exact. He was the same height, a rangy six-footer, with his father's grey eyes, long nose and pugnacious jaw. He wore his hair the same way, short back and sides, and he had the same slightly crooked, tobacco-stained teeth. I did a rapid calculation and worked out that he was also about the same age as Jack the last time I'd seen him. That helped to create the eerie illusion that had stopped me in my tracks. If it hadn't been for that, I might have bolted. Then again, there was a good reason not to move a muscle. He held a big Webley revolver in his right hand and it was pointed at my moustache.

'My old man told me all about you, Hughes. I swore I'd kill you if I ever caught up with you.'

Bluff was my only defence. 'Look, Mr Henderson, there's some mistake. My name's not Hughes. I'm—'

'Shut up!' He kept the Webley very steady as he moved towards the wall. Without taking his eyes off me, he lifted a framed photograph off a nail and laid it on the desk. 'Take a look at that, but don't touch it. Keep your hands where I can see them.'

I leaned forward to look at the photo. A flash flood of memory washed over me and swept me away. I was back in the mud and blood of the Somme with Henderson and 'Wag' Anderson and 'Spit' Thorndike and that mad bastard of an English officer, Evelyn Anthony, who nearly got me killed. This photograph was taken just after we got the news that we were embarking for France. There we were, all still in one piece with the light of battle in our eyes—well, in the eyes of some of us. The smaller men squatted in front with a pair of crossed rifles. I stood at the back alongside Jack Henderson, the lance corporal's stripe clearly visible on my sleeve. For some reason I was hatless; my dark hair was slicked back and I wore a moustache very like the one that was glued to my upper lip now. My head was circled in red ink and the words 'coward and deserter' were written above it in block letters.

The picture was twenty-eight years old, but I hadn't lost any hair or gained much weight and the 'Tazzy' impersonation had taken twenty years off me if you didn't look too closely.

'Don't pretend that isn't you.'

He hadn't shot me yet so he evidently wanted to talk. That was OK by me, though I could've done with a cigarette. It's amazing what you think of when you're seconds away from death. I shrugged. 'It's me. How's Jack?'

'He's dead.'

'I'm sorry to hear that.'

'You didn't help by bashing him on the train. He was never too good after that.'

I thought back to that event. Jack had been breathing regularly and there hadn't been much blood. I couldn't believe I'd done him a serious injury. 'I'm sorry,' I said, 'but I didn't hit him very hard. How did he come out of the war?'

'Not as well as you, you fucking coward.'

'I was shell-shocked. I wandered off. I was out of my mind for a long time.'

'Bullshit.'

It was, but there was no way he could be sure. Doubt entered his eyes for the first time.

'You had to be there to know what it was like. Your dad was the bravest man I ever saw. I wasn't brave, but I didn't desert. Not really. When we met on the train I was under a hell of a lot of pressure. Jack didn't give me a chance to explain.'

The Webley didn't move. 'What sort of pressure?'

'I was running away from my wife.'

That wasn't quite accurate, but it was close and I desperately needed something to deflect him from his purpose. His thin mouth twitched into what was almost a smile. 'I can understand that,' he said.

'I stowed away on a ship. I was a desperate man.'

He nodded. 'I hardly knew my dad. He died when I was a kid and I never met any of his army mates.'

'They were mostly killed on the Somme.'

'But he showed me that photo and he told me about you.'

'Did he tell you about how we ran the two-up games on the troopship? And what we got up to in London?'

'No.'

'Too bad. We had some times.'

'You sound like a Yank.'

'Spent a lot of time there. What's your name, son?'

I could feel him softening and I hoped the 'son' wasn't pushing him too hard.

'Bill.'

'Well, Bill, your dad was a great guy but he got me all wrong. Y'know I met him in the Liverpool camp in 'seventeen. I could tell you some stories.' I pointed at the photo. 'That's "Wag" Anderson. He stopped three machine-gun bullets in 1918. That's old "Spit 'n polish" Thorndike. He was wounded but he survived. I saw him in Melbourne after the war. That's . . .'

He put the Webley down on the desk. His eyes were brimming, so he probably couldn't have made much of a shot anyway. 'All right, all right. It was all a long time ago. I'll give you the benefit of the doubt. You can tell me a few things about Dad.'

My weakening knees stiffened. 'Sure. Be glad to. What about your mother?'

He shook his head. 'I'm an orphan.'

As soon as he spoke, he realised that it was a ludicrous thing for a man of his age to say and he let out a laugh. That broke the tension completely. He sat down behind the desk and I leaned against the wall and lit the cigarette I'd been dying for.

'Where'd you get those smokes?' he said.

I was lighting a Lucky Strike from a packet one of Ushi's clients had left behind. I held them out to him. He took one. I lit it with my Zippo and he inhaled luxuriously.

'From a friend,' I said.

'Must be nice, to have friends like that. Do you know what these are worth on the black market?'

I shook my head.

'I better not tell you. You probably wouldn't give me another one.'

We smoked in silence for a while. He really did look remarkably like his father but, as I studied him more closely, there were differences. His eyes had a shrewdness Jack's had lacked, and they were set more closely together, giving him a slightly foxy look. His movements were nervous, where Jack's had been sure and purposeful. I tried to remember what Jack's trade had been before he joined the army. I couldn't recall—something up country. Maybe that accounted for the differences; Bill Henderson was a city man if ever I saw one.

I dropped the cigarette into the hubcap that seemed to serve as the ashtray and sat on the edge of the desk. 'I was surprised to see Jack as a' train guard,' I said. 'I thought he was a country boy.'

'That's right. The family had a farm out Sofala way, but when Dad got back from the war he couldn't do the work it needed. He'd had a whiff of gas.'

I closed my eyes involuntarily. I remembered that yellow muck rolling in and the frantic scramble to get the gas mask on. 'Bloody awful. So you grew up in Sydney?'

''s right. Randwick. Wanted to be a jockey but I grew too big.'

'And what since then?'

His eyes moved uneasily and I thought I knew what that meant. *The clink—you've got the look.*

'This and that. I'm doing all right here. I was unfit for service, in case you're wondering—crook back.'

I nodded. 'We'll have to have a few beers and talk about Jack. Right now I'm interested in buying a car. I was told you might have the right sort of thing.'

I explained my needs. He was suspicious at first, but I had one of Eric's 'Porter Productions' cards to show him and he came around. We went out to the yard (he didn't suggest that I inspect the workshop) and discussed the suitability of the Standard. We haggled over the price and then over the cost of the modifications I wanted. Eventually we came to terms. I paid a deposit and he agreed to have the car ready in four days. I gave him the remaining Luckys and drove away in the Riley, vaguely uneasy about the meeting but satisfied with the business conducted.

I got back to Crown Street, after driving through another rainstorm, disgruntled and worried. I snapped at Pam, drank two bottles of beer and fell into a brown study. I'm not, by nature, a self-questioning person, but I had to wonder where my life was going. Dogsbody on a low-budget movie, looking over my shoulder for spooks, shacked up with a whore—it didn't sound too promising as I spelled it out to myself.

'Hey, grumpy guts,' Pam said. 'You want some fish and chips?'

I'm tone deaf, very close to green, blue, and brown colour blind and my hearing was slightly damaged by the artillery bombardments on the Somme, but my taste buds are in good shape. A couple of serves of Sydney fish and chips, wrapped in newspaper with plenty of salt and vinegar, comes in near the top of my list of all-time great tastes. I joined Pam at the table and we pigged in.

'What about your figure?' I said.

She chewed hard and talked right through the mouthful of fish and potato. 'Bugger it for tonight. I won't eat for the rest of the week. What've you done to yourself? You look like a spiv.'

I'd forgotten that I was still dark-haired and moustachioed. 'For the picture. Ushi likes it.'

'Do you like Ushi?'

'Sure I do.'

'Don't hurt her, Dick. She's pinning some hopes on you. I know you'll let her down, but do it gently.'

'Pam, I . . .'

She held up her hand. 'Don't say anything. I've known your type since I was fourteen. Good bloke, no harm in you, your own worst enemy, all that bullshit. From what I can see you're better than most—you take your sex straight and you haven't given Ushi the clap. But you're passing through, aren't you?'

'I guess so.'

She picked up a chip and examined it as if it was a rare fossil. 'Pass through gently, then. Leave her with some good memories and some bloody money. I want your promise.'

'I promise.'

'Good. Have you got another bottle of that beer? I'm goin' to be a devil tonight.'

We drank more beer and ate most of the fish and chips. Ushi came home soon after while we were sitting bloated and guilty at the table. She sniffed the air.

'You bastards. Fish and chips. Where's mine?'

'In the oven,' I said. 'But there's no more beer.'

Ushi snorted. 'Beer. This is the stuff to drink.' She reached into her bag and pulled out a bottle of Houghtton's white burgundy.

'Christ, where'd you get that?' Pam said.

'I had a matinee.'

I avoided Pam's eye and pulled the cork from the bottle. We all had a glass of wine. Ushi ate two chips and nibbled at a piece of fish. 'Isn't he handsome, Pam? All got up like that.'

'Handsome is as handsome does,' Pam said.

Ushi was on her second glass, a record for her. 'Oh, he does all right. Don't you, Dick?'

I was embarrassed. 'Go easy, love. You're getting squiffy.'

'Who cares? I'm going to be a movie star.'

She used an American accent on 'movie star'—did it pretty well, too. She took a big gulp of wine.

'Eric's offered me a speaking part in *Desert Storm*.'

'*Storm Hill*,' I said. 'That's great.'

The look Pam shot me was full of reproach and warning. Ushi didn't notice. She finished her glass and poured some more.

'Yeah, it's great. I'm gonna be a star. C'mon, Dicky, let's go t' bed.'

That night she may have been drunk, she may have been on the way to a big disappointment, but she made me very glad I had black gunk in my hair and a phoney moustache.

CHAPTER NINETEEN

I picked up the Standard and drove it around Ultimo for a while. It didn't have to do much, but it did have to reach a respectable speed and I had to make sure that the weakened chassis wouldn't fall apart the first time it was driven. The car passed the test and I paid Henderson the balance of the money.

'Few particulars to complete,' he said. 'I need your address.'

I gave it without thinking. I was worried about Eric Porter's suggestion that I might do the stunt of driving the car over the cliff. I'd seen it done often enough. The car is driven at something close to actual speed for a stretch, then thrown into a skid or spin. After that, the vehicle slows down and is steered in the right direction and the driver bails out. The film is speeded up to blend the three stages together.

'Signatures here and here, Dick.'

I signed, still preoccupied. I didn't really want to do the stunt, but I was anxious to cut a good figure in Ushi's eyes and to stay tight with Eric Porter. I had no plans beyond the end of this film. I might well need work on *Storm Hill* myself. I couldn't see any way out.

'Care for a drink, Dick?' Henderson said. 'You promised to tell me a bit about my old man.'

I was willing. Anything to put off the evil hour of taking the Standard back to where the filming was going on and announcing to Porter that I was ready to drive, skid and jump. It promised to be a difficult scene to shoot. With only the one car it had to be done right, not the way it is now in Hollywood, where a director can wreck ten Lincoln Continentals if he wants to.

'A drink'd be fine,' I said, and I meant it. Although my military career had ended ingloriously, I *had* seen some stiff action, and I was as willing to jaw about it as the next old soldier, providing my guard was safely up.

We drove in the Standard to the Ancient Briton hotel in Glebe Point Road, which Henderson described as 'my local'. The clientele seemed to consist entirely of wharfies and boxers. The only place I'd ever seen so many massive shoulders, cauliflower ears and flat noses collected together in one spot was in some of the harbourside bars in San Francisco. I was surprised at the size of the crowd early on a Friday afternoon.

'Strike,' Henderson said. Then, more softly, he added, 'Bludgers.'

We were both big men and we had to use our height and weight to get through to the bar. There was a lot of shouting and shoving going on and I had the feeling that the place was going to erupt into violence at any moment. We got our schooners and jammed ourselves into a corner. A good number of the men nodded to Henderson or exchanged a word or two with him.

'Can't we go somewhere else?' I bellowed into Henderson's ear. 'I can't hear myself think.'

'No, this is the right place. They'll be off to the Trades Hall building any minute. I've got a proposition to put to you.'

I drank a couple of schooners, making one dangerous, rib-bruising run to the bar, before watching Henderson's prediction come true. The men exited the pub in a pushing, shouting mass, leaving the bar occupied by only a few oldsters, a couple of sailors, Henderson and me. The staff got busy with mops and buckets and brushes and pans cleaning up the spilt beer, the spittle, the broken glass and cigarette butts. They swabbed the tiled walls and concrete floor. I'd forgotten what an Australian public bar was like—unlike any other drinking place in the world.

'Why was this the right place?' I asked, as soon as the racket had died.

'I wanted you to see that I'm well regarded around here.'

I thought of the quick nods from the bruisers and the half-drunk salutations from some of the others. 'OK, I could see that. So what?'

'How would you like to make some money?'

I was interested, but instantly on my guard. 'Say I would.'

'Real money. Thousands. Enough to get you back to the States in style.'

Right then there was nothing I wanted more. It was disconcerting to have someone like Henderson put a finger on my deepest desire. 'Keep talking,' I said.

'Hang on while I get another round.'

He strolled to the bar and I realised what a consummate actor and conman he was. He'd left me for a minute or two to chew on what he'd said. It was the sort of thing movie directors did all the time. Henderson didn't know I knew that. I chewed, but just a little. I also lit a cigarette. I took a sip of the beer he'd bought and realised that three schooners was starting to put me away. I wasn't the drinker I used to be.

'What's wrong?' Henderson said. He lit a cigarette with a hand as steady as a lamp post.

'Nothing. What's this about a proposition?'

He leaned closer. We were still standing up because there was nowhere in the bar to sit down. 'What's the most valuable commodity in Sydney right now?'

I was three parts drunk. I wanted to say love, but I said, 'Sex.'

He grinned. 'Maybe that's second. No, the most valuable thing is petrol. How're you getting yours, Dick?'

At that time, the owner of a registered vehicle got his ration tickets from the Post Office. The allowance was small. 'Well, it's rationed of course,' I said. 'I've got Eric Porter's tickets. He's got some sort of extra allowance. It's not enough but—'

Henderson thumped my upper arm, causing me to drop my cigarette onto the wet floor. I stood on it, pretending that I'd meant to discard it.

'My point exactly. Not enough. Supply and demand. Short supply plus big demand equals top price. Simple arithmetic.'

He was his father's son all right. Jack had said things like, 'Two mugs plus one mug equals one mug, because all mugs are the same.' I nodded at Henderson Junior's uncontestable wisdom. 'Your dad would've agreed with you.'

He brushed that aside. 'Yeah. Now, suppose you could lay your hands on a big supply of this in-demand item, you'd be sitting pretty, right?'

'Right, provided that you had some way to dispose of it.'

He winked. 'Who's got a big supply of petrol?'

'Er, well, the refineries, I suppose, and . . .'

'Wrong, mate. The right answer is—the Australian army.'

I shrugged. 'Obviously. And the navy and the air force for that matter.'

'We're not concerned with them. Now, the fact is that I *do* have the outlets and I have a way of tapping into the supply.'

I thought of the cars I'd seen on the road that had obviously been adapted to run on kerosene—they lacked power on the hills and blew a hell of a lot of smoke. Not to mention the charcoal-burners. I had no doubt that Henderson was right, abundant supplies of petrol at the right price would be liquid gold. As far as I could see, though, the rationing system was tightly policed. That meant just one thing.

'You mean,' I said, 'you know of a way to steal gasoline from the army.'

'Petrol,' he said.

'What?'

'You've got to call it petrol. You're sounding more like an Aussie every day, Dick, but you've still got these funny words in your head. You've got to call it petrol.'

'I can call it any bloody thing I like.'

'Not if you want to make an easy couple of thou. Do you, Dick?'

I studied his face. The long nose and the close-set eyes, the thin mouth and the jaw that was just starting to accumulate beer fat. It wasn't a face to trust. Few are. The question was, though, was it a face to fear? I thought of what he had on me—knowledge of the name I'd enlisted under, information about my desertion and subsequent misdemeanours. Could he make trouble for me? Yes, if he knew who to talk to. Did he? Unlikely. On the other hand, I had no doubt that he was cooking up a money-making scheme and I needed money very badly if I wasn't going to end up doing shitwork on Australian films, maybe tied down to Ushi. And that was the *hopeful* prospect! I made my decision.

'I'm interested, Bill. Tell me more.'

'You're an actor, right?'

'Sure.'

'Have you ever played the part of an army officer?'

'Sort of.'

'That's what this bit of business needs—a major or a colonel. Half an hour's work.'

'That's a serious offence, impersonating an officer.'

'This is serious money.'

Of course I should have finished my drink, grabbed the car keys and got the hell out of there, but I didn't. I stayed, kept drinking, and listened. The more I heard the more I was persuaded that Bill had worked out a foolproof scheme and that thirty minutes work could make me a man of means. Moralists would say, nothing good could come of a plan to get so much for so little, but most moralists you'll find have never really been in a tough spot. Anyway, their prescriptions are too simple. True, it was big bucks for little work, but it was very ticklish work.

Briefly, the plan was this: the army camp at Richmond had an enormous supply of petrol. The NCO in charge of it was an associate of Henderson's. If a high-ranking officer were to enter the camp with a convoy of trucks and certain papers requisitioning the fuel, how was a mere quartermaster sergeant to refuse him? The scheme had been put together by Henderson, the sergeant and the proprietor of a number of petrol stations in Sydney.

'This bloke's got clout,' Henderson told me. 'His brother's a judge or something in Canberra.'

'That's a bit vague,' I said.

'I'll find out for you if you're interested. The point is, he's got quite a few coppers in his pocket and he gets to know what's going on.'

In my time I'd been involved in a few schemes to get something to people who wanted it in ways that the authorities disapproved of. The item had usually been liquor—when I was a salesman for Robespierre Wine & Spirits Merchants in Australia thirty years back, and in Chicago and LA during Prohibition. I could convince myself that this wasn't so very different. The war was won, wasn't it? The army wouldn't need the fuel but you could bet they wouldn't be turning it over to the people who did. It had been bought with people's tax money, hadn't it? So to whom did it really belong? Why, the people who Henderson wanted to supply. It all made sense to me, with the help of the beer. But my experience had taught me a few things, particularly the truth of the saying that a chain is only as strong as its weakest link.

'What about the sergeant?' I asked. 'How reliable is he?'

Henderson stroked his long chin, which was beginning to sprout ginger bristles. At that moment he looked just like his father had, when Jack had been deciding on a good place for a two-up game and whether or not to use the doctored pennies.

'We'd better have a meeting,' he said.

'You haven't answered the question.'

'Best to judge for yourself. Tell you one thing, don't judge him by his name.'

'What's that?'

'Robin Barwick. Bit of a pansy name, Robin, but he's a tough bastard.'

'He'll have to be. They'll grill him over a slow flame.'

'He's up to it. Does that mean you're in, Dick? We've just been waiting for the right bloke to do the officer.'

'Have you asked anyone else? Plenty of actors around.'

'No. They're mostly poofters.'

'I'll think about it. I'd have to meet the sergeant first.'

'Right. I'll set that up and give you a ring. I've got your number. You won't be sorry, Dick.'

I picked up the keys and my hat. 'Best we don't be seen together too much. I'm going to go for a walk and clear my head.'

'Hey, how'm I going to get back to my place?'

'Your dad could walk a mile in seven minutes carrying a bag of wheat.' I left the pub, steering a more or less straight course. It's always best to have the last word when you're dealing with crooks.

Half an hour's walking through the streets of Glebe sobered me up. It was a rough area, pretty much like Darlinghurst, with lots of small cottages and big boarding houses. There were very few cars parked in the streets and the kids playing cricket, using the lamp posts as wickets, were almost uninterrupted by traffic. The shops were small and dark and the stuff in their windows looked old and faded. The pubs were doing good business. I saw the police station at the end of the street I happened to be in and I turned on my heel. I was acting like a criminal already.

I drove the Standard back to the bushy location near the Narrabeen Lakes and showed Eric Porter the modifications. He nodded knowingly, as if the whole thing had been his idea.

'Feel like doing the stunt, Dick?' he said.

Mercifully, I was in the act of lighting a cigarette when he spoke. This gave Finch time to chime in.

'I'll do it, Eric,' he said.

'Sure,' I said, a split second later.

Finch grinned. He'd been drinking a little, not too much, and he was loose. 'Unless Ron wants to try it.'

Randell was standing quietly by combing his hair, of which he was inordinately proud. He smiled and shook his head.

Porter looked worried. 'I don't think so, Peter.'

Finch turned belligerent immediately. 'Why the hell not? I've finished all my scenes. I can do it. Done it before.'

'We, ah . . . might have to reshoot,' Porter said.

Finch sneered. 'You don't have the money to reshoot. D'you want me for your next picture or not?'

Porter knew that Finch's performance was the best thing about *A Son is Born,* and that his chances of financing *Storm Hill* depended on having Peter aboard.

He shrugged. 'Talk to Dick. I'll blame him if you break your neck.'

Finch clapped me on the back. 'Nothing to it, is there? Shoot from the passenger side, driver's door half open, steer for the edge and do a dive-roll out. Right?'

'Right. The tricky part's handling the skid.'

'Steer into it. We played around a bit with the jeeps up north. Nothing to it.'

That was Finch. Sober, he was quiet and a bit unsure of himself. With a few drinks in him he was brimful of confidence with women and everything else. Of course, it was the ruin of him in the end, as with so many others, but he had a good innings. He raced off to get a pair of overalls while the props men fixed the dummy in the passenger seat and the cameras got into position.

Nowadays, when so many of the movies seem to be nothing but car chases and smashes, the little scene we filmed at Narrabeen would be very small beer. But back then, in Australia, it was something of a novelty and the whole crew gathered to watch the fun. I did everything I could think of to make it go right, including checking that the oil slick which would provide the skid wasn't *too* long or *too* slick. I also made sure there was only enough petrol in the tank to complete the run. One time in Hollywood I'd seen a stunt like this go wrong—the driver couldn't get out, the sparks started flying and the punctured fuel tank was full.

Finch did everything wrong. He stalled the car when he first started it. Then he revved it too hard and had it moving too fast when he went into the skid. The Standard slithered for what seemed like minutes and I was sure it was going to go over the bank at thirty miles an hour instead of three. Finch somehow managed to get traction and brake but he still hit the edge too fast and the car plunged over with the engine making more noise than it should. I caught a glimpse of Peter before that and he looked panicked. The Standard bounced a few times, hit a couple of trees and disintegrated. There were shrieks from the women and groans from the men. I fully expected to be in the party that scrambled down to retrieve his mangled body.

The spinning back wheels threw up some dust and when it cleared there was Finch, flashing his white teeth in his suntanned face and pushing back his hair. That's a big part of being a star— they screw up like everyone else, but things work out fine for them.

CHAPTER TWENTY

After striking my deal with Bill Henderson I jumped at shadows, grew irritable and went off my food. Life started to get tricky at Crown Street. With Ushi working on the film, Pam felt left out of things. The two women had double-dated with their American clients as often as not, and Pam confided in me that this was one of the things that had made the life bearable.

'It's not the same, solo,' she said one night when Ushi was late getting back from Narrabeen. 'Not nearly as much fun and not as safe.'

'How's that?' I asked.

'The Yanks behave better when there's two of them and two women. They're not as likely to get blind drunk and go in for the rough stuff.'

I had seen very little bad conduct by our gallant allies so I didn't take much notice. Besides, my mind was on other matters. Pam reminded me of my promise not to hurt Ushi and to leave some money for her when I left.

'I'm working on it,' I said.

Pam's normally good-natured face arranged itself into something like a sneer. 'You don't say. I'd never have guessed.'

'What d'you mean?'

'Jesus Christ, you men! You must think women're deaf, dumb and blind. Do you think I don't know you're mulling something over? How bloody illegal is it?'

'Well . . .'

She waggled a finger at me. 'Just you remember, Dicky boy. Any trouble for Ushi and I'll land you in the shit so fast you'll think all your birthdays have come at once.'

That was just what I needed for my peace of mind—an avenging angel poised to squeal on me if things went wrong.

Henderson's call came two days later.

'At the stadium tomorrow night,' he said.

'What stadium?'

'Rushcutters Bay, of course. Two ringside tickets for you at the gate.'

I said, 'Who's fighting?' but he'd rung off.

I checked the paper. Alan Westbury was fighting Jack McNamee for the Australian middleweight title. I like middleweights—you can get speed *and* punching power. It was late in the evening. Ushi and I had done a day's work on the film. Pam was out with a client. We shared a bottle of over-priced black-market beer in the kitchen. Since she'd started hanging around with the film people, Ushi had shown a little more interest in the suds. My ardour had cooled somewhat, the way it does unaccountably, but I was hot for her that night. She was wearing her silk dressing gown and I was getting a good view of her firm little breasts and her big, shapely legs.

I put my hand on her dimpled knee. 'How'd you like to go out on Friday night?'

She yawned. 'Out where?'

'The stadium, to see the fights.'

'Ugh.'

'Ringside seats. Championship bout. Bound to be celebrities there. You might meet Jack Davey.'[29]

The poison had got into her blood. She jumped into my lap and nibbled my ear. 'Oh, Dick,' she said. 'Yes, I'd *love* to go to the wrestling.'

'Boxing,' I said, but that was the last thing she got wrong that night.

It had been more years than I cared to remember since I'd been inside Sydney Stadium. The last fight I'd seen there had been Les Darcy's demolition of Buck Crouse. That had gone only two rounds of a scheduled twenty and had ended in the usual way, with Les grinning and the other bloke sleeping. When people ask me who was the best middleweight I ever saw, I can never decide between Les Darcy and 'Sugar Ray' Robinson. Mickey Walker wasn't bad.[30] I know who was the worst, a young chap who wept after being hit on the nose in an amateur three-rounder—me.

Nothing much had changed about the old barn since the days of the twenty-rounders. There was still a good deal of rusted corrugated iron in the construction on the outside, and inside the same fug of beer breath and tobacco smoke. Our tickets were waiting for us at the gate as Henderson had promised, and Ushi and I pushed our way through to the ringside section. I was surprised at the size of the crowd. The papers later gave it out as 10,000, which was a good house for a couple of pretty average pugs like Westbury and McNamee. The fact was that after five years of war, Sydney needed diversion.

Ushi was done up to the nines in a blue dress that flattered her unusual figure. She'd had her hair elaborately arranged and wore a little blue hat that wouldn't have kept off any rain, but that wasn't the point. She drew a lot of whistles as we made our way to our seats and I could see from her face that her night was made. A six-round preliminary was in progress in which no-one was very interested. Jack Davey was at ringside, looking like the king of radio in a dinner suit with his thin silver hair gleaming. Darby Munro was there too. It wouldn't matter if every fight was a schlenter, Ushi would be happy.[31]

We sat down and I looked around for Henderson and Sergeant Robin Barwick. No sign. Evidently security was being observed. I hoped no meetings in the toilet were planned—my recollection of the facilities at Rushcutters Bay Stadium was of a wet, slimy floor and a smell something like the Hun gas in France. In the ring a couple of lightweights were dancing around each other as if each was trying to make the other giddy. Nothing much happened in the way of punches. The crowd was restless but Ushi appeared to enjoy it.

'It's something like the ballet, isn't it, Dick?' she said.

The man next to her snorted and said something about cream puffs, which puzzled Ushi. She kept looking across at Davey and his entourage and touching her hair. There were a number of women at ringside, all dolled up, but none outshining my companion. The lightweight match ended in a draw, which seemed to be what they'd had in mind all along. Then an Aboriginal welterweight, all skinny legs and spidery arms, pulverised a slow-moving opponent inside two rounds. He got a shower of coins from the audience. Ushi looked concerned when the white boy had to be lifted onto his seat. The man sitting next to us wadded up a ten shilling note and flicked it into the ring. He'd won big on the fight. The Aborigine's trainer scooped the note up and put it in his pocket.

On to the main event and there was none of this blondes in a body-stocking holding up the round numbers business you see today—more's the pity. No music, no silk robes, just two tradesmen in dressing gowns, McNamee in black shorts, Westbury in white, and may the best man win. The referee was Joe Wallis, whose stomach cut off a good part of the ring. He was nimble enough to stay out of the fighters' way, though. Westbury was the heavier, indeed he looked a bit soft in the middle; McNamee looked trim, had the speed and a snappy left.

I settled down to enjoy the fight, forgetting why I was there. The smoke thickened and seemed to cluster around the ring. Again I was reminded of the gas welling up out of no-man's land and rolling towards the trenches. Ask anyone who experienced it, they'll tell you it's something you can't forget. It was a pretty good fight. McNamee was faster and sharper in the early rounds and scored with his left pretty freely on Westbury's face. Didn't seem to be hurting him much though. Westbury had a good fifth round. I remember it because I got a five quid bet down on him then with the high-roller next to us.

'He'll run out of steam,' he said, after Westbury landed heavily a few times and had McNamee holding on.

'A fiver says he doesn't.'

'You're on.'

We let Ushi hold the stakes. Around the tenth I thought I was going to lose because McNamee put in a few good rounds and was well ahead on points. Westbury wasn't doing much and his corner-men began to look concerned. A man almost as fat as Wallis spoke urgently to Westbury between rounds.

'Who's that?' I asked.

The man in front of me turned around. 'Bill McConnell. If Westbury wins he'll be McConnell's thirteenth Australian champ.'

Ushi looked at the money in her fist and shook her head.

Westbury was a changed man in the eleventh. I wouldn't say he got up on his toes, but he moved around more, hemmed McNamee in more often and got in some good shots. McNamee started to hold. Wallis used his big gut to butt him away. Westbury looked fresh. He caught his man on the ropes and landed a good combination. McNamee looked confused at the end of the twelfth but he might have got the decision if that had been the end. With three more rounds to go he didn't have a hope. He held, was belted in the clinches, got butted by Wallis' belly, was cautioned and Westbury finished all over him.

Wallis held up his hand immediately and the announcer jumped through the ropes. 'The winner and the new middleweight champeen of Australia, Al–an West–bury!'

A few boos from the McNamee supporters, but general acceptance of the decision. Ushi handed me the money. She mightn't have known much about boxing but she knew how to settle a bet. I kissed her. 'Champagne,' I said.

'Right,' said a voice in my ear. 'At Ziggy's.'

It was Henderson. He winked at me as he pushed away through the crowd.

Ushi clutched my arm. 'Who was that?'

'A friend. Let's go to Ziggy's.'

The Ziegfield Cafe on King Street was a nightclub and a notorious sly-grog joint. You could drink there until the early hours if you were prepared to pay the prices. The outrageous mark-up wasn't all profit; the management had to shell out handsomely to the police to remain in business. We shared a taxi with some other celebrants, some going to Ziggy's, others to various clubs in the Cross and Surry Hills. Ushi had been trying to keep Jack Davey in sight but she lost him. I assured her he was likely to be going to the Ziegfield, but, if the scuttlebutt was true, he was probably going off somewhere to blow his money on baccarat.

Henderson met us outside the club. There was some sort of charade about membership which involved forking over money and then we were inside. I'd been there once before with Finch, but I'd been too drunk to form any clear impressions. It was a big place, dimly lit, with a bar along one side and a lot of tables and chairs all crammed in together. There was a small bandstand with a few musicians sitting about looking as if they might eventually get around to playing something, and a tiny dance floor, but the real business was drinking and smoking. The air was like a London pea souper and Ushi started to cough almost immediately.

'I can't breathe,' she said.

'A few glasses of bubbly and you won't notice.'

Henderson was steering us to a table in the corner where it was so dark you couldn't recognise your own mother. I could tell that Ushi wanted to be out where she could see and be seen, but Henderson was in charge. We sat down; an ice bucket with an opened bottle of champagne appeared along with four glasses. I poured quickly and got a glass straight into me. Ushi sipped her wine cautiously, gazing around for a famous face. Henderson tapped her on the shoulder and gave her a pound note.

'Goodnight, miss,' he said.

Ushi's jaw dropped. 'Who do you think you are? I'm not going anywhere. Dick?'

'Tell her, Dick.'

It wasn't my finest hour. That was the point where I began to break my promise to Pam, but what could I do? I was worried. *Why hadn't we had our meeting at the stadium? What was the point of coming here?* Henderson was relaxed and I was edgy. I gave Ushi another pound. 'Sorry, love,' I said. 'Business. You'd better get a taxi.'

The look she shot me would have stripped paint. It occurred to me later that I was treating her the way some of her clients did. She showed a lot of class by simply arranging her wrap around her shoulders, standing up and walking out without a backward glance. I felt like a worm and poured another glass.

Henderson's close-set eyes, screwed up against the smoke, followed her out of sight. 'Unusual shape,' he said.

'Get fucked.'

'Listen, Dicky, we're not playing games now. It's all serious stuff from now on.'

'I'm not sure I want—'

'You've got no choice. Here're our partners, and now you've seen them you're in with no fuckin' way out.'

Two men were approaching the table. The musicians started to play but I couldn't make out the tune. The contrast between the pair was almost shocking. One was a small, nuggetty number with gimlet eyes and a rat-trap mouth; he wore a nondescript grey suit. The other was large and fleshy, soft all over and wearing a beige suit with a hand-painted silk tie. They sat down. The big man signalled for more booze and glasses.

'This is Dick,' Henderson said. 'Hughes, Kelly, Browning, whatever you want to call him. Robin Barwick and Douglas Erskine.'

Erskine was the fat one. He grinned around a big cigar. 'Let's call him the brigadier.'

Barwick lit a cigarette. 'I hear you're a deserter. If you desert us we'll cut your fuckin' heart out.'

CHAPTER TWENTY-ONE

It turned out that the terrible trio, Henderson, Barwick and Erskine, had been watching me at the stadium to make sure I had no suspicious contacts.

'The sheila's a pro, isn't she?' Barwick said.

I nodded. 'In a way.'

Erskine smiled and puffed his cigar. He'd tossed off one glass of champagne and was working on his second. Henderson and Barwick hadn't touched the wine. 'How many ways are there?'

I was starting to relax and put two and two together. Erskine had to be the publican and petrol-station owner, the guy with the clout in Canberra. He looked the part. His hands were manicured although they'd done hard work at some time in the past. Barwick was the most dangerous. If you made the effort to observe, everything about him shrieked paranoid crook, although it would be easy just to overlook him altogether. But he'd be the enforcer if one was needed. Henderson appeared to be the planner and co-ordinator. Erskine emptied the champagne bottle and called for more. Henderson ordered beer for himself and Barwick. I could have done with a scotch, but I settled for some of the fat man's champagne.

'So you've established that I'm not a phizz,' I said.[32] 'What next?'

'Not much,' Erskine said. 'Just wanted to look you over. You'd be a forty regular, wouldn't you?'

'That's right,' I said. 'Might need an extra half inch in the leg. Got a good tailor on the job?'

'Good enough.'

'Shit,' Barwick said.

Erskine turned his mild eyes on him. 'What's the matter with you, Robin? The man's perfect, can't you see that?'

The antagonism between the two was something of a comfort. I leaned back in my chair and lit a cigarette. The band, now noticed, was playing 'Begin the Beguine' and a few couples were dancing. I almost felt like taking a turn myself. Winning money and drinking champagne does wonders for the spirits. With the music and the noise of conversation, laughter and bottles touching glasses, there was no danger of our talk being overheard.

'I would like to know a few more details,' I said. 'Such as when and how.'

'Soon,' Henderson said.

Barwick drank some beer. 'How's not your worry.'

'Now, now,' Erskine said soothingly. 'The man's got a right to know. Briefly, Brigadier, you'll be in charge of a convoy of ten lorries that will load about 1500 gallons of petrol.'

'Who'll do the loading?'

'The soldiers.'

'Who'll do the driving?'

'Other soldiers,' Erskine said. 'From . . . other places.'

Barwick looked disgusted. He rolled a cigarette and lit it with a Ziegfield Cafe book match, dropping the matches into his pocket. Erskine reached over and removed the folder. He placed it on the table. 'Careless, Robin. Very careless.'

It was clear then that Douglas Erskine was the brains behind the whole thing. Somehow, that didn't make me feel any better.

Back at Crown Street, Ushi had locked her door and I had to sleep alone. I tried to apologise in the morning but she was very cool. I wished I still had the use of the Riley so I could offer to drive her to work, but Porter had reclaimed it. The shoot was almost finished, but they needed a busy street scene and Saturday morning in Neutral Bay was the place to get it. Ushi, in a dark wig, was playing a shop assistant with one line. 'May I help you, madam?' She was excited about it and pretending that I didn't exist. Pam was still in bed with a fat US major.

I was slightly hungover and in need of comfort. Ushi would just have time for a quick one if I could persuade her. Maybe I could get a car out of Henderson on loan. Banking on that, I proposed a picnic for Sunday. Ushi looked up from her boiled egg.

'Where?'

'You say.'

'Watson's Bay.'

Just the mention of the name gave me a start. It was where my film career, such as it has been, got its start. I spent a couple of hours up beyond my balls in cold water as an extra in one of the innumerable versions of *Mutiny on the Bounty* and then got robbed by a Maori actress and landed in Long Bay gaol. The place didn't have happy associations for me.[33] Still, I was out to curry favour not to please myself, so I agreed. Ushi beamed, kissed me and put on her hat.

'Er, Ushi, how about . . .'

'No time, Dick. Tonight if you're lucky. I'll put on the lacy stuff.'

So I had to be content with that. It really wasn't such a bad prospect and, of all the women I've known, Ushi was the quickest to recover her good humour. It's a great quality, and if I'd had any sense I'd have . . . but there's no point in might-have-beens. I moped about for the rest of the day, helping the major into a cab, cleaning up the mess he'd made in the bathroom and rebuilding my bridges with Pam. She wasn't having any.

'You're a wrong 'un,' she said. 'Ushi cried her eyes out last night. The soooner you're gone the better.'

I stormed out and ran straight into an insane woman in Palmer Street who was handing out white feathers to every man over five foot and under sixty. I spent the day in a rage and committed my first serious illegal act on Australian soil—on that particular visit, I mean. I was somewhat under the influence when I arrived at Henderson's car yard in Ultimo, and I didn't let his absence or the locked gate stop me. Five minutes later I was driving away in a hot-wired Buick convertible with white wall tyres and leather seats. I calculated that when Ushi saw the car she'd climb into her lace frillies for sure. I was right.

Sunday promised to be a scorcher. The sky was milk white and there wasn't a breath of wind. Pam, with her redhead's complexion, tried to dissuade Ushi from going to the beach.

'D'you want to turn into one of those old handbags on legs you see around town?'

'My skin tans,' Ushi said. 'Like Dick's.' We were back on very friendly terms by this time.

'Tans! Listen to yourself. Tanning is for leather.'

We ignored her, packed a hamper and set out along Old South Head Road. I explained the wires bristling out under the dash-board as an electrical experiment, a test to see whether a radio could be installed in the car. Ushi was a great fan of radio quiz shows and dance music programs—the explanation was aces with her. She looked very fetching in a sundress and sandals with a wide-brimmed straw hat and open-weave cotton gloves. You have to be my age or thereabouts to remember how ridiculously people togged themselves up in those days. I was wearing a modified tennis out-fit—cream tousers, open-necked shirt and a sleeveless pullover, even though the temperature was in the nineties. We bowled along, cre-ating our own breeze, and arrived at the beach in high spirits.

I hadn't seen the place since I'd crawled from the water to collect my extra's pay, and I was astonished at how much it had changed. Gardens had replaced the scruffy foreshore, the fishermen's shacks had gone along with all the rusting boats and rotting jetty. The streets were lined with substantial houses and the old hotel had gained some extensions and a considerable facelift. I parked down near the water. We arranged our picnic under a tree and hopped down to the beach for a swim. That sort of thing was possible then—now, if what I read about Sydney is true, you'd come back to find your hamper and blanket gone and call yourself lucky if you still had your shoes and socks.

After our swim we ate sandwiches, drank beer, did some very discreet canoodling and fell asleep. I awoke covered in sweat with flies buzzing around my eyes. The heat was intense and I fanned myself with one of Ushi's magazines. As I did so I had the odd feeling that I was being watched. I stopped fanning and looked around. All over the little piece of parkland people were clustered under the trees. Most were asleep. No one was looking at me. I lit a cigarette and gazed out over the dark blue water. Still no breeze. The yachts in the harbour were moving sluggishly in the currents. The feeling would not go away.

Ushi woke herself up with a slight snore. 'Ooh, sorry. Fan me, Dick, there's a dear.'

I fanned her, still looking anxiously around. Ushi was too relaxed to notice. I drowsed and when I woke up again a dark cloud had covered the sun and a breeze had sprung up. A fat raindrop fell on Ushi's face and she jumped to her feet.

'It's going to pour. Come on!'

We barely made it to the car in time. I struggled to get the roof up as the thunder rolled across the sky and the rain came sheeting in from the east. The water fell in buckets and the car wouldn't start. I cursed, fiddled with the wires and finally got it to kick over. We were parked on a dirt patch that was rapidly turning to mud beneath us. The wheels spun but I managed to get enough grip to move the Buick slowly onto the tar. It was like being in a carwash; the water flowed across the windscreen. I turned the wiper knob and nothing happened. I tried the lights and the horn. Same result. I stopped and a blast of protesting horns sounded all around me.

'Why've you stopped? I want to go home.'

'I've stopped because I can't see. The wipers aren't working.'

'Well, *make* them work!'

'I can't.'

'I *have* to get home.'

'Why?'

'I've got a customer tonight.'

It may sound surprising, but I was shocked. I stopped fiddling with the knobs and wires and looked at her. The water on her face wasn't rain. She was crying. I reached over for her but she pulled away. The horns kept blowing but I ignored them.

'I thought you'd . . . given that up,' I said. 'I thought Eric was going to put you in the next picture.'

She sobbed and beat her fists on the dashboard.

'With these tits and these legs and this bum? Are you kidding? Get this bloody thing moving.'

There was misery in every sound and movement she made. I couldn't think of a thing to say. I climbed out of the car into the deluge, wound down the window and pushed until I got us to the side of the road. I got back in, soaked and shivering. Ushi was huddled in the corner staring at the flooded windscreen.

'I'm sorry,' I said.

She sniffed. 'It's not your fault. I was a fool to think things could be any different from what they are.'

'Things *can* be different. I—'

'Shut up, Dick. You'll be off soon, I know. Well, I've beaten you to the punch.'

'What d'you mean?'

'I'm going to work for Reggie Stuart-Jones.'

'The abortionist? You're crazy. He just got one bullet in him this time. Next time he'll be chopped liver.'[34]

'He's got protection.'

'Sooner or later he'll kill some poor girl and you'll be up with him for murder. Or, more likely, just you. He'll be in London or Paris.'

She turned on me fiercely. 'What would you know about it? Don't tell me you haven't paid for a few backyard jobs in your time. If you'd seen what I have—girls bleeding to death, leaking pus, blown up like whales. At least he's a doctor and knows what he's doing. At least he washes his hands and uses clean instruments.'

She was right. I knew nothing about abortion. That was more due to luck than good management. I could see the sense in what she said, although it still sounded risky. But who was I to be advising someone to watch out for the law? I asked her where she'd met the doctor and she told me—at a nightclub a 'client' had taken her to recently.

'When you were away cooking up whatever scheme you've got in mind. I've talked to Pam.'

That'd be right, I thought. *Reggie Stuart-Jones and nightclubs went together like ham and eggs. He even owned a couple of the bloody things. And once a whore, always a whore.* These thoughts didn't make me feel any better. I said nothing and we both sat there miserably, waiting for the rain to stop. It did at last. I wiped steam from the windshield and did the few things I know to do to cars—dry the distributor, prime the carburettor and so on—and got the Buick moving.

Nothing was said until we were driving along Riley Street towards the vacant lot where I usually parked.

'That car's following us,' Ushi said.

'What car?'

She pointed to the rear vision mirror, which had been knocked a little askew by my wire fiddling and windshield wiping. A dark green Morris saloon was behind us, keeping its pace to ours.

'The green one?'

'Yes. It followed us all the way from the beach.'

'Shit. Why didn't you say something sooner?' I went past my parking lot.

'I wasn't sure until we started turning corners. Don't snarl at me. Who is it?'

I bit back another snarl and wondered what to do. Your honest citizen drives straight to the nearest police station and hollers for the boys in blue, but I could hardly do that. It's a little unlike me, but my thoughts were as much for Ushi as for myself. As one who has known a good deal of disappointment, I could feel hers almost as a tangible thing. I didn't want to add physical injury to it. I stepped on the gas, made some sharp turns and pulled up outside the house in Crown Street.

'Jump! Get inside quick!'

'Dick, what . . .'

I shoved her hard. 'Just go!'

She hopped out, scooted across the pavement and was inside almost before I could get moving. The Morris had made use of the time though and it was hard behind me. I accelerated down Crown Street, pushing the Buick through the gears without a clue in the world of what to do. The Morris stayed with me easily. For all its flashiness, the Buick lacked power. I soon found that it also lacked tyre tread; the roads were still wet after the rain and the first turn I took at speed almost piled me into a wall. I fought the wheel, got control and found myself heading for Oxford Street, where I hoped there'd be more protective traffic. The Morris driver wasn't having any of that; he shot past me, leaned on his horn and crowded me into the kerb. I hit the brakes, skidded, bounced against the high gutter and came to a shuddering stop.

The engine stalled. I groped for the wires but the passenger door was jerked open and Robin Barwick leaned inside. He put a pistol to the side of my head.

'Get out, you stupid bastard. Get out now!'

I gasped for breath. Having the business end of a gun poked into your ear can have all sorts of unsettling effects. 'Barwick. Robin. What's going on? If you wanted a talk you could have . . .'

He grabbed a handful of my wet shirt and jerked hard. I slid across the seat and got out of the car. Bill Henderson was standing on the pavement looking at the Buick.

'I can explain, Bill.'

'Shut up.'

There was a laneway near where we'd stopped and Barwick dragged me towards it with a bit of an assist from Henderson. My feet slipped on the wet flagstones but there was no resisting them. Barwick, though small, was incredibly strong. Henderson was angry. They propped me up against a wall and Barwick put his pistol away.

'Don't hurt his face,' Henderson said.

Bugger that, I thought. *Don't hurt any part of him.* Stupidly, I put my hands up to protect my face and Barwick punched me in the stomach. I felt my picnic lunch heave. Then it settled and he hit me again. I started to slide down the wall, still shielding my face, and Barwick crashed a couple of hooks into my ribs as I went down.

'You are a stupid prick,' he grated. 'With everything at stake you go farting around with a whore in a stolen car. What if the coppers had stopped you?'

He emphasised the question with a kick that landed somewhere near my kidneys.

'Easy,' Henderson said.

'I was going to return it,' I gasped. 'How did you find out anyway?'

Another kick. 'Someone saw and heard you, you dumb shit. A big, dark bloke who said 'goddamn' in a Yank accent when he had trouble with the lock. It didn't take much to work out who it was.'

He kicked me again, this time in the ribs, and the pain shot through me, making me gasp.

'That's enough, Robin,' Henderson said.

'I'd like to shoot your nuts off,' Barwick said.

I was sitting down by this time, with my bum getting wet through the seat of my pants. I couldn't be sure that I hadn't pissed myself. Barwick grabbed my hair and pulled my head up and back. He took a piece of paper from his pocket and stuffed it into my mouth.

'Get out of that bloody whorehouse tonight. Go to this address and wait. Do what you're told, when you're told, or you'll be sorry and then you'll be dead. Understand?'

I nodded, fighting for breath.

He let go and dusted off his hands. I slumped back against the wall and watched them walk away down the alley. I pulled the paper from my mouth and immediately vomited. The mess went over my trousers and feet. The smell made me throw up again and again until I was retching dryly. I heard the cars start up and the engine noise die away. Lying there, I was visited by an image of myself collapsed in an alley, covered with blood and vomit, hoping to die. I had trouble placing it until I started to shiver. The temperature had dropped suddenly and I was cold in my wet clothes. All at once I was back in Butte, Montana, derelict and close to death among the trash bins outside the Copper Club. It had been a very low point in my life and I'd sworn never to drop down that far again.[35] I dragged myself up and began to hobble in the direction of Crown Street.

My progress was slow and I drew a few curious looks. I didn't care. I limped along in my wet, soiled clothes, cursing Bill Henderson, the army and the Commonwealth of Australia. I reached the door of Ushi and Pam's house and fumbled my key from my pocket. I was just about to put it in the lock when a voice hissed at me from the next doorway.

'Dick. Christ almighty, man, is that really you?'

I squinted at the bundle of rags. They parted and a bespectacled face peered up at me. The face was gaunt but still rounded, the eyes were slanted. It was Harry Kaminaga.

CHAPTER TWENTY-TWO

I blinked and knuckled my eyes. My ribs and stomach were sending waves of pain through me every time I moved, and now this! I thought I was suffering from a spinal injury causing brain damage.

'It can't be you,' I croaked.

'The fuck it can't. It *is*! Get the door open so's I can stop trying to look like a trash can.'

I opened the door and Harry was around me and inside before I could take a step.

'Thank the living Christ! This is the first time I've been under a proper roof in three weeks.'

'What're you doing here?'

'What do you think? I escaped. You owe me. I'm here.'

'How?'

'Now that's a hell of a story. Hey, this isn't a bad place. You screwing both of those chicks?'

'You've seen them?'

'Sure. They took off not long before you arrived. Would there be anything to drink? Hey, Dick, you don't look so good.'

'Good of you to notice. I've just been bashed.'

'Robbed?'

'No. It's a hell of story.'

Harry grinned. There was something about him that impelled you to tell jokes, make light of things, which isn't my natural inclination, especially if I'm in pain. I took him through to the kitchen and found a bottle of Hennessey brandy contributed by an American officer. We both got two stiff tots into us before doing any serious talking. Harry was almost literally dressed in rags—old tennis shoes with holes big enough to pass the balls through, tattered khaki overalls held together by bits of string, and a jacket that might once have been black but was now a whitish green. His hands and face were filthy, which reminded me of the state I was in.

The house had two bathrooms for obvious reasons. We both got cleaned up and I found some pants and a shirt for Harry. He had to roll the cuffs and sleeves up a foot or so, but he looked better as a clown than a scarecrow. My ribs weren't broken and the pain had settled to a throb. I was bruised from armpit to waist on both sides and all movements had to be made gingerly. I took some more brandy for medicinal purposes. Harry was looking thin, but not too bad for someone who'd been sleeping rough for weeks.

'I was as fat as a pig when I took off,' he said. 'They worked us in the camp but holy shit the food was good. Never eaten so many lamb chops in my life.'

'So why did you escape? I thought you wanted to sit the war out. It sounds like you had it pretty cushy.'

'I wouldn't say that. Some of the guards were proper bastards—but the other prisoners were the real worry. It wasn't no Coney Island. But the reason I scrammed was my story was looking a bit thin. A couple of airmen came in and they knew something about the kind of flight we were on. My story about being the only survivor and so on didn't sit too well with them. They started to ask questions about the crash, the condition of the plane and so on. I stalled, pleaded loss of memory, but they were about ready to start in on me with the bamboo skewers.'

'How did you get to Sydney? How did you find me?'

'By freight train, how else? I travelled all over California riding the rails. It's a cinch. I stole the clothes and stole what food I could. That wasn't so easy. Lucky this place has great weather.'

I was starting to put a positive construction on Harry's arrival. I was in a very bad spot with Henderson and Co, and a resourceful ally like Harry had to be a plus. Of course, there was always the drawback that he was a Japanese, with whom we were locked in mortal combat. All in all though, I was glad to see him. I poured him another brandy and fixed us both a huge club sandwich.

'Harry,' I said, 'there's a couple of million people in Sydney. I'm delighted to see you, but how did you find me?'

'Sheer, dumb luck,' he said, around a mouthful. 'I hit town yesterday. Slept in a park. I was walking along this Crown Street looking for some place to steal food when I saw you pull up and throw the broad outa the car. Then you took off with that green car after you. I hung around, figuring maybe I could talk to the woman. Then they lit out and you arrived. Luck, like I say.'

Harry finished his sandwich and picked up the crumbs with a moistened fingertip—a sure sign of someone who has been on short rations. Suddenly I gave a yelp and dashed from the room. I had remembered the scrap of paper I'd stuffed into my pants pocket. I'd left the trousers in a crumpled, wet heap on the bathroom floor as was my habit. If the ink ran and I couldn't read the address ... I came back smoothing out the paper. The writing was blurry but still legible. Harry poured himself another drink and leaned back in his chair.

'So, Dick, tell me what's been happening with you. Did you ever get to make that movie?'

There was probably no need for me to tell him everything but I did. For one thing, it helped me to get it all in perspective and make up my mind what to do. For another, if Harry was counting on me to help him it was wise to let him see up front just what kind of spot I was in myself. He listened, helping himself to the brandy and waving away my cigarette smoke.

'How much is in this gasoline deal for you?'

'A few thousand, if I live to collect it.'

Harry whistled. 'That's useful dough. With that, we should be able to get on a boat back to the US of A.'

'What are you talking about?'

'Dick, Dick, there's no future for us here. Our one chance is for you to pull this job and scoot.'

'What's this "us" and "our" stuff?'

'You owe me, Dick. Remember the snake.'

'I'm in a jam myself, Harry. I'm in no position to help you.'

'The fuck you're not. A coupla grand'll buy us tickets to South America and more. But for now, you need someone on your side if these pals of yours get nasty. I've been in the Japanese army, buddy. I can get nastier that your cheap hoods could imagine.'

Put like that, I had to agree. I imagined Robin Barwick's reaction if he came face to face with Harry in a dim light. I knew where I'd put my money. I placed the piece of paper on the table.

'Room Ten, Dowling House, Kings Cross,' Harry read. 'Some kind of flophouse?'

'Bet on it,' I said.

I packed up my meagre belongings and stole a few things from the house—a US army captain's shirt that fitted Harry better than mine and a pair of shoes ditto. We took the rest of the brandy and a bottle of gin, as well as several packs of cigarettes and some tins of coffee. I made sure to pack the .45 I'd taken from the Yank officer. The Americans were our benefactors in those days, no mistake. I considered leaving Ushi a note but decided against it in the end. I had no money to leave so I'd well and truly broken my promise to Pam. I reasoned that the less Ushi knew about me and my future movements, the better for her own health. Convenient reasoning perhaps, but there you are.

I've done some mad things in my time, like kidnapping that murderous bastard Pofirio Calderon, putting my fists up against Errol

Flynn and placing myself under the direction of Eric Von Stroheim, but tramping through the streets of wartime Sydney in the company of an escaped Japanese POW has to rank as one of the craziest. Nevertheless, that's what I did. Harry and I walked to Dowling House. He wore a hat pulled down over his face and dark glasses. Being a Japanese, he couldn't grow much of a beard and the bit of stubble he'd acquired in the past three weeks only served to make him look more disreputable.

It made no never mind at Dowling House. I soon learned that it housed people who made Harry look like a stockbroker—gaol-breakers, army deserters, ship-jumpers of all nationalities and descriptions. The place was run by a man named Lew Phillips, who charged low rents and took a cut of the jobs his residents pulled. It was an early example of criminal organisation in Australia. Phillips was in touch with people like my backers who needed a place for the executive branch to stay and for certain goods to be stored. For these services he received commissions. He was very thick with certain members of the New South Wales police force, some of whom he paid in cash and some with information. He was playing a very profitable but very risky game, was Lew.

I was expected and had no trouble booking my mate, 'Chow' Casey from San Francisco, into an adjoining room. I knew the information would get back to Erskine, Barwick & Henderson (I was starting to think of them as a business partnership which might not be too concerned about its record as an employer), but it couldn't hurt to keep them guessing just a little. Harry and I settled into our rooms, which were small, hot and dirty, his a little more so than mine. We sat in my room, looking out over the wet rooftops, and I gave him a very edited version of how I'd managed to get myself into the present pickle. I stressed my friendship with Finch and played down the brief brush with Oliver Featherstonhaugh.

'Seems to me your movie buddy has to be of some use in getting us outa the shit when the time comes.'

'I can't see how. Peter's not the type to fall over himself doing things for other people. If convenient, fine, otherwise it might just be too much bother. Besides, he was up in Darwin when your lot bombed the bloody place.'

'It wasn't me, pal. Still, I get your drift. How about the broad?'

'I want to keep her out of it.'

'Sir fuckin' Galahad. Did you say the hoods reckon the job's on soon?'

The thought made me scramble for the brandy. 'That's right. Soon.'

'Leave me think about it. First things first. You're gonna have to get me some clothes, Dick. Plus I need a shave and a haircut.'

'Can't do much today. It's Sunday. Everything's closed.'

'I noticed that. How does a man get a drink?'

'You don't, unless you buy a meal.'

'Christ, and they call us barbaric. Is everyone real religious, or what?'

'I think it's got more to do with trade unions than religion.'

Harry nodded. 'Dangerous things, trade unions. I remember one time when I was grape-picking in the valley—'

The door opened and the space was entirely filled by a man. He must have stood close to six and a half feet and he was built like a telephone box. His forehead was low and beetling; his nose was flat and he had the worst pair of cauliflower ears I'd ever seen. He was wearing a singlet and I could see that, although his muscles were covered in fat, they were still big muscles.

'A quid each,' he grunted.

It was a surprise to discover that he could actually speak.

'What?' I croaked.

He cracked the knuckles on one huge, red hand. 'A quid each. I'll make it a fiver if you get cheeky.'

'What for, ape?' Harry said.

I stood up, ready to apologise for him, but the monster brushed me aside. He moved into the room and loomed over Harry, who was still sitting on the bed.

'What did you say, Chink?'

Harry stood up slowly and looked at me in mock astonishment. 'Didn't you tell Lew my name was Chow? I don't like to be called Chink. I don't like it at all. Especially when it's a gorilla talkin'.'

I was thinking of diving under the bed for the .45, but things moved way too fast for me. The gorilla lunged for Harry but Harry wasn't there. He glided away and found a little space between the bed and the wall. It was a small space for his opponent but enough for Harry. The gorilla came at him again and Harry moved his feet and hands in a co-ordinated shift that looked slow and effortless, but was in fact lightning fast and packed with power. He landed with kicks to the knee and groin and followed up with a couple of elbow jabs and a heel-of-the-hand chops that brought the big man tumbling down like a demolished chimney stack.

Harry sniffed and flexed his hand. 'Didn't quite time it. I might get a bruise, godammit.'

I breathed out slowly. 'How the hell did you do that?'

'Ancient Japanese art, brother. It's not all scroll painting and cherry blossoms in old Japan, I can tell you.'

I was suddenly very glad to have Harry on my side. Things seemed a lot better. I felt sure he could handle Erskine and Henderson and a few more besides. I remembered how he'd felled me back in the Japanese camp in the Queensland bush. It had felt like a hammer blow but was obviously a love tap. Harry removed a wallet from the hip pocket of the man who was lying with his trunk collapsed over the bed. The wallet was stuffed with notes.

'Greedy bastard,' Harry said. He took several notes and stuffed the wallet back. I hadn't seen him take it, but a driver's licence appeared in his palm. He unfolded the greasy, sweat-stained paper.

'Leonard McGregor,' he read. 'Ever heard of him, Dick?'

I had. 'He was a wrestler. Now he's a standover man, an enforcer.'

Harry looked down at the unconscious McGregor. 'I don't understand this country,' he said. 'Guy here doesn't seem to me to have the qualifications for that line of work.'

CHAPTER TWENTY-THREE

The next day I went out and bought Harry a razor and a pair of scissors. He went into the bathroom and came out looking considerably less Japanese. He'd straightened his peaked eyebrows and given himself a basin cut that made his face look fuller and softer. The clothes I bought at his instruction had a slightly Chinese look, too—a dark jacket, rather long, white shirts with high collars and trousers a bit narrower than was fashionable. Togged up like that he was unrecognisable as Sergeant Haruki Kaminaga. As Chow Casey from San Francisco, he looked mild until you felt his hard, black eyes on you. Then, if you had any sense, you minded your manners.

It surprised me that Harry was happy to wander around the Cross and the Woolloomooloo docks and go into town. He seemed to have no fear of being spotted. His disguise was good, but his behaviour seemed reckless to a cautious soul like me and I tackled him about it.

'You read anything in the papers about an escaped Jap POW, Dick?'

'Now that you mention it, no.'

'You bet your ass, no. See this?'

He showed me a recently healed cut on his upper arm.

'Did that getting through a barbed-wire fence. Bled like a pig. Too good an opportunity to miss.'

'What do you mean?'

'I was only a day away from the camp. I guessed they'd be look-ing for me but keepin' it quiet. Wouldn't want to spook the natives. I laid a bit of a trail to a railway bridge. Then I took off my camp shirt and soaked it in blood. I left it on the bridge. Hell of a drop to the water and the river was real shallow just there, though it got deeper further on. You jumped, you'd break your neck for sure. I snagged one of my socks on some branches a bit downstream and, hey presto, one dead Jap! Neat, huh?'

I agreed but, like a lot of feerless men of action, Harry tended to see only what he wanted to see. Privately, I had reservations. What Harry had said was right—the authorities wouldn't want news of an escaped Japanese POW getting out. Which meant that there was no way to tell whether or not they'd been taken in by his trick. I hoped so.

Two days went by and there was no contact from the firm. I was beginning to hope that they'd found someone else to play the part of the officer. So much so that I was thinking of quitting Dowling House. That would take money. I phoned Eric Porter, partly to claim some wages, partly just to see what was going on.

'Dick,' Porter said. 'Where've you been? I've been trying to get in touch with you.'

I considered that statement. Porter owed me money, he wouldn't be trying to make contact for that reason. Maybe Ushi . . .

'I've been busy, Eric. Has Ushi . . .?'

'Haven't heard from her since I gave her the news about *Storm Hill*. I tried to break it to her gently, but she took it hard.'

'I know. Er, Eric, I'm due a few quid. I wondered if you could . . .'

'I'll hand it to you personally at the party. If you don't come you don't get it.'

'What party?'

'We've finished filming. There's a party at my place tomorrow night. I really want you there, Dick. You did a tremendous job, especially with the car. That scene's a beauty.'

'Thanks, Eric. Well, sure I'll come. Can I bring a friend?'

'Like that, eh? You move fast. Well, I know Ushi won't come, so why not? Eight o'clock.'

I hung up, feeling encouraged. Porter owed me a fair sum and if Peter Finch was flush, as he sometimes was, I might be able to hit him for a loan. Also, Ron Randell owed me twenty pounds on a bet. When we'd been doing our mock New Guinea sequences, I'd said something about a sniper shot we were filming being too easy.

'Easy?' Randell had sneered. He'd never had much time for me, seeing me as a mate of Finch's who was stealing the picture. 'It's the best part of a hundred yards.'

'Seventy at most,' I said carelessly. 'Too easy.'

'You could hit a target like that yourself, I suppose?'

Randell scarcely knew one end of a firearm from another, and had taken badly to Finch showing him how to hold his Owen gun.

I squinted at the set-up. A sniper in a tree had to take the slouch hat off a soldier standing motionless in a clearing. 'I could do it three times out of three.'

'Twenty quid,' Randell snapped.

I took the bet, got hold of some live ammo and climbed the tree with a Lee Enfield .303. They put a hat on a stick and I knocked it off three times. Shooting's one of the few things I've ever been good at. I'm better at it than winning money, but this was one of those lucky times when someone underestimated me. It didn't happen all that often.

So there were good reasons to go to the party. Harry was getting a little edgy, wanting to know when the job was going to be pulled. *A party'd be good for him*, I thought.

'Any chance of getting laid?'

'Some. More than around here, unless you want to pay for it.'

'OK, I'll come. But I'm telling you, Dick, unless these pals of yours get in touch pretty soon, I'm going to have to ask you to come up with some other scheme.'

'Meaning?'

'We need dough. You've got a piece. I've seen it. I'm getting some very bad ideas.'

'Harry, I've been in the gaol they've got here. It's a very nasty place.'

'Think positive, Dick. This town is leaking money. It's just a matter of having the right mop.'

I closed my eyes. *So much for camaraderie.* Now I had to think about scraping as much cash together as I could to get away from Harry! It was enough to make me wish I'd followed my mother's instructions to get a good, safe job in the public service where you wore a suit to work every day and had a pension to look forward to.

I've been to more end-of-filming parties than I've had screen credits, and in my experience they all follow the same pattern. Whether they're held in London, Sydney, Los Angeles or Colombo, they start out with everyone loving everyone to death and saying what a fabulous job was done by all hands. As the booze gets to the participants, the facade starts to crack.

'She was really hopeless in that scene. They had to do twenty takes and it still wasn't right.'

'He was too pissed to stand. That's why they shot him sitting down. I admit it worked, but really . . .'

'The picture has to work. His last one bombed and if it wasn't for, well . . . you know, he'd never work again. I know it for a fact.'

Harry and I arrived at Porter's house while the kisses-all-round were still in full swing. My policy at these affairs is to find the big names early and make my obeisances then, just in case I get into an unfit state later on. I left Harry in the kitchen with Jane Holland and located Muriel Steinbeck and John McCallum and congratulated them. Gracious acceptance. Then I hunted out Randell and extracted my twenty. He was well on the way to being soused and paid up cheerfully.

'I say, Dick,' he said. 'D'you think I was all right?'

'You were great, Ron. You've got a big, big future.'

He squared his shoulders. 'Yes, I'm sure I have.'

Poor fool.[36]

I was introduced to a Doctor someone and a Mrs somebody else who goggled at me the way filmstruck people do. I was polite. I wandered around the small rooms for a while, chatting to this person and that and soaking up the booze. The party was soon going full swing. The rug was rolled back in the living room and people were dancing in the non-athletic but romantic way they did in those days. The smoke and noise were mounting and I asked Porter if he anticipated any trouble with the neighbours. I was thinking ahead. The thing Harry and I needed least was contact with the police.

'No fear,' he said. 'Women on both sides. They're here. Promised I'd introduce them to Finchy.'

I hadn't even bothered to try to approach Peter. He was surrounded by women the whole time. No sign of Tamara, and I concluded he was making hay while the sun shone. Eventually there was a break in the traffic and I was next to him against a wall. He was panting slightly from a bit of the two-step—never as fit as he looked, our Peter.

'Dick,' he roared. 'Where've you been hiding?'

He was as drunk as W.C. Fields on a good night. His eyes were glassy and the hand holding his cigarette looked as if it was about to start directing the New York Philharmonic.

'I've been around, Peter. Got a few deals cooking. You know.'

'I don't bloody know,' he said belligerently. 'I've got nothing fucking cooking. Have to get out of this bloody country soon's the war's over. You too, Dick. You too.'

My sentiments exactly, but sooner if possible. 'How's Tamara?' I asked.

'Away dancing somewhere.'

A tall bottle-blonde in a tight red dress grabbed his arm and pulled him away from the wall. His slack, self-pitying expression changed to one of ardent interest as he picked up the beat and slipped into an easy foxtrot. There never was a man like Peter Finch for doing what was expected of him.

I danced a decorous rhumba to Guy Lombardo with Muriel, and just as well it was sedate because my ribs were still sore from the beating. Then I went out onto the balcony for a smoke. Strange how we go out into the fresh air to pollute ourselves. There were a few people standing around, leaning against the rails and getting their second wind. I lit up, tossed the match out into the void and stared towards the water. Suddenly, I heard Harry's chuckle. He'd come out onto the balcony with a short, fat man who was having trouble keeping upright. Harry steered him to a beer keg that was a casualty of the festivities. If I hadn't known better I'd have thought Harry had sexual designs on his companion. He kept his arm around his shoulder longer than was necessary and bent over solicitously so as not to miss a word he said.

I strolled over. 'Having a good time, Chow?'

'I'll say I am.' Harry straightened up and winked at me. 'I want you to meet someone, Dick. This is Harvey Beaumont. He's a doctor, aren't you, Harv?'

It was the doctor I'd met earlier. 'Specialist,' he said. 'Ear, nose 'n' . . .'

'Throat,' I said.

'Right. Throat.'

Harry held a white business card in his hand. 'Harv is thinking of making a trip,' he said.

I nodded. 'Always a nice thing to do.'

'Harvey owns a yacht,' Harry said. He jerked his head, indicating that I was to leave. I muttered something about getting another drink and sloped off. Harry kept working, staying in close, filling Dr Beaumont's glass with champagne. He laughed, talked earnestly, then scribbled something on the back of the card. Inside, the party was livening up. There were more dancers and some of them were shouting the words of the songs. Another beer keg had been tapped and the glasses were being filled and emptied rapidly. I couldn't see Finch, but the blue jacket he'd been wearing was still draped over the back of a chair.

'Looking for Finch?' Ron Randell's hair had fallen out of its customary backsweep and was lying tangled down across the top half of his face. He was very drunk.

'Not really,' I said.

Randell pointed to a door. 'In there. Two women. D'you really think I was good?'

No matter how much I drank I couldn't seem to find the mood. By midnight I was ready to leave and I went looking for Harry. I found him helping the fat doctor down the stairs. Eric Porter was holding the door open.

'Give me a hand, Dick. Taxi's coming.'

We bundled Beaumont into the cab and said our goodbyes and thanks to Porter. Harry whistled as we walked towards the ferry. He took the card from his pocket and examined it.

'The *Macquarie Belle*, thirty-footer. How's that sound?'

'Small.'

'That fat quack's our ticket outa here,' Harry said.

We talked about it on the ride back to the Quay and Harry convinced me that it was feasible to leave Australia on the yacht in wartime. I forget his arguments; I was too drunk to follow them. Harry's head was crystal clear. He hailed a cab and shoved me in.

'You go to the flop and pack our stuff. The boat's moored at Rushcutters Bay. I'm goin' to take a look at it. With a bit of luck we can get aboard tonight.'

Drunk or sober, I was all for getting out of Dowling House. I gave Harry some money and got out of the cab in the Cross. The streets were busy. Well-dressed, well-heeled Americans were swarming in and out of the nightspots and women clung to their arms, enjoying their easy charm and generosity. Bitter-faced Australian soldiers in their heavy, graceless uniforms glared as the Yanks swanned past them. A signals sergeant spat into the gutter as a black GI walked by, high, wide and handsome, with a freckle-faced redhead on his arm. Two of his mates forcibly restrained the sergeant from making a more violent protest.

I turned into the street and approached Dowling House, thinking of other times I'd used boats to get out of tight spots—the *Sternwood* to leave Australia in 1919, the *Darwin* to escape from the LA rum-runners a few years later.[37] Two figures, one short, one tall, blocked my way.

'Hello, Dick,' Robin Barwick said. 'We've been waiting for you.'

CHAPTER TWENTY-FOUR

There was nothing to do but go along quietly. I thought longingly of the .45 under the mattress, but who takes a gun to a wrap party? They bundled me into the back of a big Dodge. Henderson did the driving. Barwick did the quiet, menacing part. The only thing to do was pretend enthusiasm. I lit a cigarette and puffed on it aggressively.

'So, when do we go?'

'Tomorrow,' Barwick grunted.

'I hope the uniform fits right.'

'Shut up.'

So much for chumminess. We drove west for an hour. Barwick let me smoke one cigarette. When I attempted to light another he took it from my mouth and threw it out the window. It was an uncomfortable drive. The suburbs fell behind and we were in open country. My knowledge of the geography west of Sydney was virtually nil. We were somewhere between the Blue Mountains and the sea. The lights of a small town were visible and I caught sight of a river as we turned off the road onto a dirt track. Henderson put the Dodge's powerful lights on high beam and maintained a steady pace. A kangaroo bounded across the road and there were several thumps as we hit other small, live things.

A few more turns, with the tracks getting rougher, and we approached a high gate. The Dodge stopped. Barwick got out and opened the gate. We went through into a large open area with sheds arranged around two sides. I saw the words 'Apples and Pears' on the side of one of the sheds as we drove past it. We stopped in front of a low building in which a dim light was shining. Off to the right, looming up in the dark against the moonlit sky, were the massive shapes of ten trucks.

I was sober now, very sober, also scared. It's amazing how young you can feel when you're having fun and how old when you're not. My bones cracked and my muscles creaked as I climbed out of the Dodge. 'Where are we?'

'Near Richmond,' Henderson said. He jerked his thumb in the direction we'd come from. 'Base's that way.'

I rubbed my hands, feigning enthusiasm. 'Jolly good. Well, what have we here?'

For an answer Barwick shoved me hard in the middle of the back, not far from where he'd recently planted his boot. 'Cut the bullshit. Get in here. We've got some talking to do.'

I took a step towards the lighted shed. My brain felt as if it was revolving inside my skull and I tried to calculate the angles. I could see figures moving around near the trucks. Ten trucks, at least the same number of men, a space like this—the investment in the job had to be large. And who was the lynchpin? No-one else but yours truly. I judged my distance, swivelled, kept my balance and swung a hard right into Robin Barwick's stomach. Maybe the punch landed a bit lower. The breath left him in a rush and his knees buckled. I shifted stance and hooked at his jaw with a left. I missed, but got him a good clip on the ear. Henderson stood rooted to the spot. I blew on my knuckles as Barwick hunched over, trying to stay on his feet and covering up against another punch.

'We'll talk,' I said. 'But you bastards need me and you'd better be nice.'

I strode towards the shed. Henderson trotted after me.

'You shouldn't have done that. Robin's a good hater.'

I thought of Errol Flynn. 'So am I.'

The fibro shed had some decrepit furniture, a fly-spotted light bulb and a number of fruit cases stacked against the walls. I sat down on the solidest chair and lit a cigarette. 'I want some coffee.'

Henderson gaped. 'We haven't got any.'

'Get some!'

'That might take a while, Dick.'

'Get on to Erskine. He's got clout, you said. He should be able to fix it.'

Barwick staggered through the door with a pistol in his hand. His normally high-coloured face was chalk white. 'I'll kill you, cunt.'

'Bang goes your petrol if you do.'

He sagged against the wall and cocked the pistol.

'He's right, Robin,' Henderson said.

'He's a piece of shit.'

'Six foot two and a half, moustache and the voice of a gentleman, guttersnipe,' I said. 'Trot out the uniform and let's hear the plan. No, on second thoughts, I need a sleep. Where're my quarters?'

Henderson reached out and lowered Barwick's gun with the flat of his hand. 'Take it easy, Robin. There's too much at stake. Maybe I should ring Doug.'

'No,' Barwick snapped. 'We'll handle it.' He advanced on me and put his pistol in his waistband. 'You can have a sleep, Browning. We'll fix you a shakedown in one of the trucks. You'll be real comfortable, and in the morning you can tell us all about your Chink mate.'

I tried a masterly sneer, but I fancy it didn't quite come off.

'Don't get things wrong,' Barwick said. 'We can call this thing off if we have to. And if that happens, your miserable life isn't worth a cat turd.'

Nice turn of phrase he had, Barwick. I was genuinely exhausted and opted for a dignified silence. They wrangled for a while as I smoked my last cigarette. Then Henderson escorted me out into the dark. I took a long piss into the grass, had a swig from a water canteen and climbed up into the back of one of the trucks. A private soldier holding a flashlight handed me a blanket and a rolled up greatcoat. He pointed the light at a folded tarpaulin lying on the floor. 'You can doss down there, mate.'

I put the greatcoat down as a pillow, took off my jacket and shoes and rolled myself up in the blanket. The night was warm but I wanted the comfort of the rough wool. I lay there listening to the noises of the night—rustling in the grass, men coughing and grunting, the barking of dogs. I couldn't sleep and crawled to the tray, thinking that I might drop down and make a run for it. A soldier with a blanket over his shoulders was sitting against the rear wheel of the nearest truck. He saw me and raised his rifle in a silent salute. I slunk back to the makeshift bed and tossed and turned until I eventually fell asleep. When I woke up the sun was high in the sky and the back of the truck was like a sauna. I was drenched in sweat and itchy from whatever had been biting me for most of the night. I swore and scrambled down.

'Gidday,' the flashlight-holder from the night before said. 'Fancy a cuppa?'

'Coffee,' I said.

He shook his head. 'Don't know about that, mate.'

Barwick and Henderson were standing beside the shed. In the daylight the original function of the place was obvious—it had been a collection, storage and loading point for fruit. There was even a fruity smell in the air which I hadn't noticed at night. I hitched up my trousers, worked my shoulders and strolled across towards my 'partners'.

'Gentlemen,' I said.

Henderson offered me a cigarette, which I accepted. 'We've got you some coffee, Dick.'

'Good. I'll need a wash next.'

'No problem. We've got everything laid on.'

Barwick spat into the dust and walked away.

Over the next few hours I drank coffee, got cleaned up and was briefed on the plan. All this was courtesy of Henderson who, I assumed, was acting on instructions from Erskine. Barwick kept out of my way. He was dressed in his army uniform and spent most of the time being unpleasant about the appearance and condition of the trucks. The sky was cloudless and there was no wind. The yard began to smell more and more of rotting fruit and the flies were ferocious. There were plenty of reasons for tempers to fray and Barwick appeared to be taking advantage of all of them.

The scheme was pretty simple. I, as Lieutenant Colonel Ian Marshall, was to head up the truck convoy due to arrive at the Richmond army base at 1830 hours. My orders were to carry away 10,000 gallons of petrol and Quartermaster Sergeant Barwick was to OK the transhipment.

'I know Barwick likes to think he's the top dog,' I said, 'but there must be officers in the place he should refer to.'

Henderson shook his head. 'Matter of timing. The CO won't be there; the 2IC will be off screwing some woman in Richmond and the other officer will do whatever Barwick tells him.'

We went over it until I had all the moves off pat and was absolutely clear on the timing. Barwick turned up around midday looking hot under the collar and nervous. He was carrying a pressed uniform—shirt, jacket trousers, shoes, the lot. He put them on a chair after brushing away the dust.

'Thanks a lot, Robin,' I said. 'Looks good.'

Barwick bustled forward like an angry bull. I gave way until he had me backed up against a wall. He needed a shave, his eyes were red and his breath was foul. 'I don't like you, Browning. I don't like anything about you. I was all for calling this off and getting someone else, but I've been overruled. So you're right, we need you for the operation. But maybe you've already blown it.'

'What d'you mean? I haven't—'

'One question. Did you tell that bloody Chink anything about this job?'

'No,' I said. 'Not a word.' An absolute lie, of course, but I couldn't have survived all the vicissitudes I had so far if I hadn't been able to lie convincingly. And it wasn't as if a light of hope would spring into my eyes at the mention of Harry's name. I hadn't known the location of the army base when I'd told him about the heist, and he had no way of finding me or of doing anything to help.

Barwick glared up into my eyes. Lucky I had a big height advantage on him. If I'd been any closer to that stinking breath I might have passed out. 'OK,' he said. 'But remember this, if you put a foot wrong I'll cut you down.'

He meant it and I could see how it would work.

'Hey, there!' Barwick shouts as I attempt to wriggle out of the business. He shoots me and the trucks get clean away in the confusion. Brave Sergeant Barwick gets a medal for foiling a dastardly robbery. Ne'er-do-well actor Dick Browning lies dead in the dirt clutching a batch of forged army papers.

'I'll play it straight,' I said.

Barwick eased himself away. 'You better. Now let's go over it all again. I have to get back to camp.'

At 1600 hours I was sitting in the cab of the front truck. I was sporting my colonel's uniform and was all spit and polish. The orders were in a briefcase on my lap. My mouth was dry from nervous smoking all day and my nerves were stretched tight. I needed a drink badly but Henderson had forbidden alcohol for all hands until the job was over.

'Then you can get as pissed as you like. You'll be able to drink that French stuff. Don something.'

'Dom Perignon,' I said.

'That's right.'

That sounded fine but I had grave doubts about my ability to drink anything once we'd got away. Dead men don't drink. These morbid thoughts filled my mind as the truck bounced along the track. The driver was a thin-faced corporal who'd suffered badly from acne not many years before. I tried to engage him in conversation to take my mind off my uneasy bowels, but he responded only in grunts. The convoy and its team looked utterly convincing to me. The trucks were dusty; the soldiers had that blend of slackness and efficiency the army induces. They were a mixture of old and young, unremarkable. Men doing a job. My uniform fitted perfectly and sheer terror had caused me to get my lines off by heart. Perhaps the thing was going to work.

I fingered my Sam Browne belt and felt the weight of the side-arm, a BSA .45 revolver, unloaded, and about as much use as a breadstick. It was like one of those nightmares—when you're placed in front of an orchestra with a baton and can't read a note of music, or when you're back at school, sitting for a maths examination, and you have trouble with the four-times table. I sweated into the collar and armpits of the starched shirt. I felt like an imitation man, as if my moustache was stuck on and my teeth were false and my swagger stick was really a knitting needle.

'Gates,' the driver said. 'Got your pass?'

Suddenly I was calm and controlled in the head, although my guts were rumbling. I felt fatalistic, resigned. I could do it all, and maybe everything would be all right. Maybe the terrible trio would pay up and Harry and I could sail into the sunset on the *Macquarie Belle* with Dr Harvey Beaumont. Hold that thought.

The soldier at the gate snapped to attention when he saw me. I handed him one of the papers from the briefcase and he told the driver where to take the truck. We rolled through the gate. I glanced back and saw the other trucks following without hindrance.

'So far, so good,' I said.

The driver ignored me. He swung the wheel and brought the truck to a stop in front of what looked like an aircraft hangar. I looked around and noticed that the army base had an aviation feel. Away to the distance, in the fading light, I could see a windsock hanging limply from a high pole. The air was hot and heavy and I sweated harder as we lost the breeze created by the moving truck. I climbed down and looked around, feigning boredom the way officers do. Officers, unlike other ranks, get a lot of help in doing their job. The trick is to expect it and exploit it. The hangar was actually a huge Nissen hut. As I stood there, slapping the soft briefcase against my leg, a small door opened in the front of the building and Robin Barwick stepped out. I could hear the other trucks pulling up behind me and I took a few casual steps towards the sergeant, who hurried across the space between us.

He snapped a salute. 'Good evening, sir.'

I returned the salute languidly. 'Evening, Sergeant. Colonel Marshall, Brigade HQ, Nowra. Orders to collect some fuel.' I took my time unzipping the briefcase and extracting the papers. I passed them to him with a slightly shaking hand but managed to avoid dropping my swagger stick.

Barwick examined the papers. 'Yessir. I'll get a detail to load the drums, sir.'

I turned away. 'Do that, Sergeant. Hot, isn't it? Any chance of a cup of tea?'

This was a code to establish that the coast was clear.

Barwick responded as anticipated. 'I'll see what I can do, sir.'

He turned away and began bellowing orders to the men who had followed him out of the hangar. A large door rolled up and several fuel drums were rolled out. My driver dropped the tray of the truck and slid down a loading ramp. Barwick and I watched while the first drum was rolled up into the truck.

I heard a footfall and a metallic click close behind me. I spun around to stare into the barrel of a Thompson sub-machine gun.

'I think that will be quite enough, Dick.'

The man speaking and holding the Thompson was 'Oily Feathers'.

CHAPTER TWENTY-FIVE

It was Douglas Erskine, of course, who had sold us out. Featherstonhaugh's team had Robin Barwick and the drivers wrapped up in a matter of seconds and he told me all about it as we were sitting in the otherwise empty officers' mess. That might sound chummy, but I was wearing handcuffs, which detracts from the chumminess.

'Erskine has been on our books for years. Got into trouble initially for talking to the wrong people.'

It seemed a long time since I'd met any *right* people. 'What kind of wrong people?'

'Russians, back when they weren't our allies. They won't be once the war is over, you'll see. Can't pal up with Communists, not when you've got friends in high places. Well, Douglas agreed to work for us instead, or, rather, as well. Follow?'

I grunted and lifted my coffee cup in my manacled hands.

Featherstonhaugh was enjoying himself. 'Ordinarily, this petrol business would have been a police matter and I suppose Douglas would have done business with them. But then your name cropped up and he put in an enquiry to us.'

'And you were delighted, Oliver. Promised him a knighthood.'

'He'll probably get one anyway, in the fullness of time. That sort of chap. But don't flatter yourself, Dick. You were just small beer. Put my interest down to the old school spirit.'

'Revenge, you mean.'

'Precisely.'

'Wouldn't have a drop to put in this coffee, would you? I've been dry all day and I could do with a shot.'

He took a hip flask from his pocket, unscrewed the silver top and poured a modest measure of what turned out to be whisky into our cups. I took a reviving sip and, the way it often does, the mere taste of liquor stimulated my brain.

'Hang on,' I said. 'You said I *was* small beer—past tense.'

'That's right. Until you harboured an escaped Japanese POW.' He shook his head. The plastered-down hair stayed perfectly in place. 'Consorting with the enemy. Tch, tch. Serious matter.'

I took a gulp of the spiked coffee. 'How did you find out about Harry? Have you got him?'

'Matter of watching and waiting. Too right we've got him, though I have to admit he damaged a couple of our men in the process.'

'Good.'

'I wouldn't take that tone if I were you. Your neck's about two inches out of a noose.'

'Bullshit.'

'Depends what we make of it, old son. Now, suppose Kaminaga's an enemy agent and you're his contact . . .'

'You're joking. He was on a plane that crashed in Queensland.'

'So you say. Sounds a bit thin, don't you think? A Jap who speaks perfect English. Hiding out with you in a thieves' den and masquerading as an American while you steal a huge cache of petrol, possibly for sabotage purposes.'

I was speechless. I gulped down the coffee and held out my cup for more whisky. Featherstonhaugh added a few drops. 'What was it you used to call me at school? You and the other big fellows? I seem to forget.'

I said nothing.

'Come on, Dick. Let's hear it.'

'Oily Feathers.'

He laughed. 'That's it. Oily Feathers. Well, look at us now. You're on your way to gaol, and do you know where I'm going?'

'I don't give a shit.'

'No, because that's the kind of bastard you are. But I'll tell you anyway. I'm off to see that whore girlfriend of yours. I think I might be able to come to some kind of an agreement with her.' He stood and signalled to a beefy character leaning against the door. 'Take this man away!'

It was a low point. Being in gaol always is, whether it be in Australia, the United States, Britain or Ceylon. I should know, having experienced them all. Ceylon, I'll have to admit, was worse than average. Still, Parramatta gaol was bad enough. Just the look of the massive stone walls sent a chill through me, which is what the architecture was designed to do, no doubt. To my relief, I was put in a single cell. There's nothing worse than having to fight off some hairy brute who's spent so long admiring his own dick he thinks it only natural that others should admire it too.

Truth to tell, I was exhausted after the events of the past few hours. It's not every day you go on a big heist, get caught, run into an old school chum who hates your guts and get threatened with execution as a spy. Very taxing. I pissed in the smelly, seatless toilet bowl and washed my hands and face at the enamel sink. I stripped off most of the smart uniform, lay down on the hard cot, pulled the thin blanket up around my shoulders and drew my knees up towards my chest. In my experience, you can sleep any way you like in a soft bed with satin sheets when you've got an amiable companion and a skinful of good booze. On your belly, back, either side, makes no difference. But in gaol, tired, frightened by what *had* happened and fearful about what *might* happen next, the foetal position comes naturally.

I woke up early. Gaols are like hospitals in that respect, which is one of the reasons I hate both institutions. The hawking, coughing and spitting, the banging of metal on metal and the groaning, grunting and cursing marked the morning in Parramatta prison the way it probably does in Vladivostock and Addis Ababa where, thank God, I haven't had the pleasure. An orderly brought around a bucket of stewed tea and a bowl of something that looked like grey soup.

'What's this?' I said, accepting the bowl through the cell bars.

'Weeties, Yank.'

'I'm not a Yank.'

'Then ya should know what Weeties is.'

It was a kind of cereal—flakes, presumably, at some earlier time. The addition of powdered milk and a long wait between preparation and serving had turned it into a tasteless mess that had to be prised off the spoon with the teeth. I was hungry so I ate as much of it as I could. I also slurped up the tea, a drink I loathe.

They're getting to you, Dick, I thought. *Already you're doing things you don't want to do.*

Exercise time came and went and I wasn't invited to join in. This was puzzling—was I being treated as a special privileged case, or being denied my rights? I was climbing the wall with tobacco craving and shouted and raved, having nothing to bang against the bars after the breakfast things had been removed. No response. I used one of my smart officer's shoes, but it had a rubber heel and the noise it made barely carried beyond my cell. Remember, I wasn't exactly a young man and I'd been subjected to a good deal of pressure. As the morning wore on I became desperate. A couple of prisoners in the section were returned to their cells. One of them told me to shut up and lie down.

'What d'you mean lie down? Where are all the others?'

'Workin'.'

'Why aren't you working?'

He chuckled. 'It's Saturday, mate. I'm a Seventh Day Adventist.'

I slumped down on my cot and made a silent vow that, if I ever got out of this, I'd go back to the Church of England.

I was there for three days, only being released from the cell once, to have a shower. My uniform was taken away and I was issued with prison clothes that itched. I was given some tobacco on the second day and it felt like Christmas. I made polite enquiries about being charged with something or the possibility of seeing a lawyer, but I received impolite replies. I'd seen enough movies to know what you're supposed to do in prison—stay tough and silent, do push-ups and sit-ups, meditate, keep a diary. Not one man in a hundred can do these things. I certainly couldn't, I sat on my bed, smoked and fretted.

'Prisoner! Out!'

The door swung open and I stepped tentatively from the cell. It's surprising how quickly the cell becomes like a home, a place where at least you're safe and things are predictable—it'll be the same spider today as yesterday, the water will drip into the sink in the same way. I'd heard a few quick bashings being administered at odd times and I was reluctant to leave the safety of the four close walls. I was also desperate to get out, of course. The guards escorted me down a couple of passageways into an office that oddly resembled my headmaster's study at Dudleigh—same panelled walls and heavy furniture, books in glass cases. Featherstonhaugh was there, wearing his smart suit but not the accustomed smirk. He was sporting a nasty black eye.

What-ho, I thought, *something's gone your way, Dick.* I dropped into an armchair, the first soft thing I'd had my bum on in three days, and looked at him.

'There have been developments,' he said.

'I'm glad to hear it. I've been held illegally, denied my rights—'

'Shut up!'

He was edgy and I searched for a way to exploit that. There was a cigarette box on the desk and a heavy lighter. I leaned over, flipped the box lid, took out a smoke and lit it. Featherstonhaugh opened his mouth to protest but thought better of it. He lit a cigarette of his own and paced. He scratched at the crown of his head and the carefully oiled hair stood up in spikes. I smoked and said nothing; when someone's doing such a good job of working himself over, there's no need. Eventually, he stopped and took a folded piece of paper from his breast pocket. He slapped it down on the desk and thrust a fountain pen at me. From the look on his face he was wishing it was a bayonet.

'Sign this!'

'What is it?'

'You can read, can't you? It's the Official Secrets Act.'

I leaned back in my chair, took a last drag on the cigarette and butted it. I picked up the paper and scanned it. Mumbo jumbo, but the gist was clear. Sign that paper and everything you'd done from the age of ten on became a state secret which, if divulged, got you locked away forever. I put the paper on the desk and shook my head.

'You bloody well sign it. I already have, you idiot.'

I looked at him. He was white around the mouth but the rest of his face was bright red, and with the shiner and the hair sticking up he looked for all the world like a Rosella parrot. 'Do you mean, Oliver, that you're recruiting me to work for your outfit? I'm flattered, but I think I'll refuse. No good at that sort of thing.'

'What on earth are you talking about? This is just a way of keeping your miserable carcass out of prison and I'm a very reluctant messenger, believe me.'

That was abundantly clear, but old Ollie also liked the sound of his own voice, so he went on to tell me how the Americans had found a use for Harry Kaminaga—something to do with their operation in the Philippines—and Harry's price for cooperation had been a clean bill of health for yours truly. I was touched.

'You won't believe this,' Featherstonhaugh said, 'but that miserable little Jap said of you, "He's a white man." The nerve of some of these bloody people.'

I laughed until the tears came, then I laughed some more. Good old Harry, he'd know better how to get up the noses of stuffed shirts like Featherstonhaugh than any man alive. The fountain pen was sitting on the desk. I picked it up and unscrewed the cap.

'If I sign this, what then?'

Oily Feathers sniffed. 'No charges against you over this incredibly stupid petrol business, and you never breathe a word to a living soul about it, me, Douglas Erskine or Kaminaga.'

'Is that it? No compensation for wrongful arrest and imprisonment?'

'Don't press your luck. I've got a suit of clothes for you and a rail ticket from Parramatta to Sydney.'

I held the pen poised over the paper. 'How'd you get the black eye, Ollie? Ushi give it to you?'

He touched the bruise and winced. 'No, that redheaded bitch she lives with!'

You can draw and quarter someone for just so long. I signed with a flourish.

CHAPTER TWENTY-SIX

I've broken that agreement now by setting this down. But it was nearly forty years ago on the other side of the world and I don't believe anybody is still watching. If they are, good luck to them. Extradite me. I've often wondered what became of Harry Kaminaga. My guess is that he made a hell of a lot of money during Marcos' time in the Philippines, and got out while the going was good. Sydney wasn't Manila, but it wasn't hard to find good-paying work there in 1945 and I tried my hand at a number of things at which I'd had some experience—my old trade of wine and liquor selling, the used-car game, hotel security. I didn't stick at any of them for very long.

Nothing much was happening in the movie business. Eric Porter abandoned his plans to make another feature when *A Son is Born* failed to make money.[38] I had the occasional drink with Peter Finch, but his head was full of plans to move up and on and he had no need to take anyone with him.

I earned money, rented a flat in Elizabeth Bay, found women and didn't try to get in touch with Ushi. None of my intentions towards her had been honourable and she was better off without me. But I happened to be having a drink one night in March with a reporter who was attending the trial of the men who had shot Reggie Stuart-Jones. Out of curiosity and with nothing better to do, I went to the court the next day. The trial was a showcase of Sydney's criminal class and I saw Ushi from a distance—one of the many women dancing attendance on the doctor and his associates. Her clothes managed to suggest the nurse as well as the mistress. With crims, in those gun-happy days, the two roles weren't so far apart.

A hand touched my shoulder. I turned to find Pam, resplendent in a white fox fur, glaring at me.

'What the hell are you doing here, Dick?'

'I don't know. Just part of the show, I guess. How's Ushi?'

'A lot you care. She cried over you.'

'I'm sorry. I broke all those promises. But I got into a sticky situation . . .'

'Fuck you. You sicked that nasty little spook on to us.'

'I didn't! I was glad that you bopped him!'

She grinned and a corner of the tough mask peeled away. 'You heard about that?'

'I saw the shiner.'

She blew on her knuckles. Light danced on the surfaces of her rings. 'The best punch I ever threw. Piss off, Dick. If Reggie lasts another couple of years, Ushi and me'll be fine. If he doesn't, look for us up the Cross. We'll show you a good time if you've got the brass.'

Stuart-Jones was still prospering ten years later. I never saw Ushi or Pam again.

The Americans dropped the bomb and the war ended. Like everyone else who wasn't bedridden, I was out on the street in Kings Cross dancing and drinking and hugging everyone in sight. One of the people I hugged was a tall blonde woman clutching a champagne bottle. *War's really over,* I thought as I abandoned the neck of the bottle and reached for a soft part of her anatomy.

'Dick! Dick Browning!'

I hadn't noticed that the blonde was attached to a fat little guy wearing a dinner suit and holding an even bigger bottle of champagne. He slopped wine into a few cups being held out towards him, but then he thrust the bottle at me.

'Harvey Beaumont!' he yelled above the singing, horn honking and glass breaking. 'Don't you remember? At Eric Porter's party.'

'Oh, yes.'

The blonde's attention seemed to be equally divided between me, Harvey and the champagne.

'What happened to Chow?'

A quick swig on the bottle and squeeze of the blonde. 'Who?'

'Your Chinese mate. At the party. I had to put off my cruise.'

It all came back to me. Harry, Rushcutters Bay, the *MacQuarie Belle* . . . Harvey Beaumont handed the champagne bottle to someone and a space cleared on the pavement. He gripped my arm harder and pulled me down so I could hear him shouting.

'I'm leaving in a couple of days for LA. Conference on wholebody nuclear radiation. A cruise. Penny's coming, aren't you, Penny?'

The blonde flashed a smile.

'Want to come along, Dick? We need another hand.'

Fireworks burst overhead. A fire-engine siren sounded. There were cheers as a man and a woman broke into a wild dance in the middle of the street, bringing cars to a shrieking halt.

I leaned down and bellowed, 'I'm your man, Harvey. When do we sail?'

NOTES

1. See *Browning PI*, pp. 137–9.
2. Browning's memory is astray. On 18 June 1941, world heavyweight champion Joe Louis fought light heavy-weight Billy Conn in New York City. Conn surprised the experts by out-boxing the champion. Conn was leading on points when Louis knocked him out in the thirteenth round. Louis' remark was made prior to the rematch in 1946, two years after the events Browning describes here. Louis won the second fight convincingly, stopping Conn in the sixth round.
3. Flynn delivers the line in the movie *Desperate Journey* (1942), in which he played an airman operating behind German lines in Europe. For Browning's lifelong antago-nism towards Errol Flynn, see *Browning PI,* pp. 1–4.
4. See *'Box Office' Browning*, pp. 84–108.
5. See *'Beverly Hills' Browning,* pp. 39–96 and *Browning Takes Off*, pp. 9–93.
6. See *Browning Takes Off*, pp. 93–111.
7. The lines are from A.B. 'Banjo' Paterson's Australian bush ballad, *Clancy of the Overflow.* Unusually for Browning, they are quoted accurately, suggesting that he looked them up when he was recording this part of his memoirs.
8. For Browning's career in the 1st AIF, including name changes, see *'Box Office' Browning,* pp. 61–83. John

Herbert Dillinger, 1903–?, was a bank robber who became public enemy number one in the United States in the mid-1930s. Dillinger may have committed dozens of robberies as well as engineering prison escapes and other crimes. The claim that FBI agents shot and killed him in 1934 outside the Biograph Theatre in Chicago is doubted by historians.

9. For Browning's hatred of William Morris 'Billy' Hughes, see *'Box Office' Browning,* pp. 117. Robert Gordon Menzies, conservative Prime Minister of Australia from 1939–41, had favoured the export of Australian iron to militarist Japan, some of which was returned in the form of bombs and bullets. 'Pig Iron Bob' was chalked and painted on Australian walls and bridges by left-wingers.

10. A hand-rolled cigarette.

11. Soldiers' slang meaning easy or comfortable. The word entered military vocabulary in India from the Hindi *khush,* meaning pleasant.

12. See *Browning Takes Off,* pp. 168–90.

13. A schoolyard game in which players contended for the possession of an object, usually a ball. Rules are few and the game usually ended in a wrestling match.

14. See *Browning PI*, pp. 3–4.

15. See *'Box Office' Browning,* pp. 1–43.

16. George Raft, 1895–1980, appeared in many Hollywood gangster films. An ex-boxer and dancer, his most notable part was as the coin-tossing hoodlum Guido Rinaldi in Howard Hawks' *Scarface* (1932). Raft, who was alleged to have connections with real-life criminals, apparently never outgrew this role, either in his screen career or in reality.

17. In the 1932–33 Test cricket series, the English fast bowlers directed their attack to the leg side with the intention of injuring or intimidating the batsmen.

18. Presumably, Browning means to refer to the line from Wordsworth's 'My heart leaps up'—The Child is father of the Man.

19. *Smith's Weekly,* a magazine which offered a mixed diet of political and social comment, news, satire and humour.

20. Directed by Charles Chauvel and released in 1940, this film romanticised the campaign of the Australian Light Horse in the Sinai desert in World War I. It enjoyed huge success in Australia and won respectful notices overseas, particularly for the scenes depicting cavalry charges.

21. Southwell's three Kelly films were *The Kelly Gang* (1920), *When the Kellys Were Out* (1923) and *When the Kellys Rode* (1934). For Browning's involvement in the first of these, see *'Box Office' Browning,* pp. 144–54.

22. *A Son is Born* was Eric Porter's first and only feature. Later, Porter was the producer of Australia's first animated feature-length movie, *Marco Polo Jnr. versus the Red Dragon* (1972). See Andrew Pike and Ross Cooper, *Australian Film 1900–1977,* Oxford University Press, 1988, pp. 266, 343.

23. Finch played Oscar Wilde in the 1960 Ken Russell film *The Trials of Oscar Wilde.* Browning's reference to Ceylon raises the intriguing possibility that he may have been associated with the 1954 film *Elephant Walk,* in which Finch played opposite Elizabeth Taylor, who had taken the role over from Vivien Leigh. The transcription of later tapes may throw light on this matter.

24. See *'Box Office' Browning,* pp. 20–1.

25. See *Browning PI.*

26. See *Browning in Buckskin,* pp. 15–6 and *Browning PI,* pp. 206–7.

27. William Desmond Taylor was a film director who was shot dead on 1 February 1922. The killer was never found. Mabel Normand was an actress, one of the many with whom

Taylor's name was linked. The investigation of Taylor's death revealed much of the seamy side of Hollywood at the time—drugs, sexual deviation and blackmail. Many scurrilous stories about Taylor and Normand circulated and no doubt it was one of these that Browning related to Ushi.

28. See *'Box Office' Browning,* pp. 82–3, 210–11.

29. John Andrew (Jack) Davey, 1910–59, was a New Zealander who came to Australia in the early 1930s to work as a scriptwriter and singer. He made several records, but achieved extraordinary success as a compere of radio quiz shows. An expert ad libber, he commanded a radio audience of half a million at the peak of his career. Davey was an enthusiastic sportsman, gambler and nightclubber.

30. For Les Darcy see notes to *'Box Office' Browning*; for Mickey Walker see *Browning in Buckskin*; for 'Sugar Ray' Robinson see notes to *Browning PI.*

31. Darby Munro was a successful jockey then at the peak of his long career. He had won the Melbourne Cup on Sirius the year before and would win again on Russia in 1946. A 'schlenter' is a fixed fight.

32. Phizz-gig, a police informer.

33. See *'Box Office' Browning*, pp. 18–22.

34. Dr Reginald Stuart-Jones was an abortionist, sly-grog merchant, playboy and 'sportsman'. Born in London of Welsh/Scottish parents, he arrived with them as a migrant to Australia in 1912. An outstanding student, he won private school scholarships and graduated in medicine from Sydney University. After working as a GP he set up as a specialist in gynaecology. Working as an abortionist brought him a large income and into associations with criminal identities. He owned nightclubs, managed boxers and was involved in fixing horse races. He survived an attempt on his life in October 1944, a few months before Ushi Tanvier entered

his employment. In 1960 he was presented with a large tax bill and offered his customary explanation—that his conspicuous disposable income came from punting. He died suddenly of a heart attack in 1961. See David Hickie, *The Prince and the Premier,* Angus & Robertson, 1985, pp. 135–8.

35. See *Browning in Buckskin,* pp. 62–7.

36. Ron Randell was born in Sydney in 1918. He was a child radio and stage actor and had a long career in British, American and European films and television. Most of his work, however, was in supporting parts.

37. See *'Beverley Hills' Browning,* pp. 199 ff.

38. Browning is mistaken. Porter's film was not released until 1946 and according to film historians it achieved 'solid results'. Porter abandoned *Storm Hill* and returned to making documentaries and commercials, presumably for more pressing financial reasons. See Andrew Pike and Ross Cooper, *Australian Film 1900–1977,* 1980, p. 266.